KU-356-354

Created for podcasting as *Tom Corven* 2005
Revised for print and renamed Dreamwords 2010

Cover design by Paul Story

www.dreamwords.com

UK English

Book One in the Dreamwords Series

Dreamwords

by

Paul Story

The Honesty Edition

I am indebted to *The Friends of Tom Corven* who pre-ordered a $500 Special Edition of this novel in the belief that Dreamwords would be successful. While the money helped, their support and encouragement was invaluable too. Through them and through family and friends, I raised the capital for this venture. To those people, especially to those who have not met me, I owe a debt of honour. Their extraordinary trust in supporting a stranger half-way across the world has allowed me to bring this to you in such an unusual way.

Thank you…

Jim and Sandra
Steve and Rhonda Jones
Illustrativeman
Ventsislav Zhechev
The Ohmann Rowe Clan
Paul Coombs
Mark Francis
Brian Telfer
Jean and Kari Kilgore
Brendan O'Neill
Julian Procter
Ann-Marie and Jim Leith
John Simnett
Bruce Wright
liz1073
Matilda

Dreamwords started life as Tom Corven, the world's first novel written for podcasting. A short introduction to a major work, this edition has been renamed and revised for print. Its author asks a simple question:

Should the Dreamwords Series be Published?

There is no conglomerate behind this project, no large corporation picking up the tab or providing a safety net. This book is brought to you directly by the author with the support of family, friends and fans.

If enough readers enjoy the first book and enough of those are honest and pay for it, I will publish the next in the series.

Sometimes, it seems to me, that marketing is about tricking people into buying things they neither want nor need. We've all bought books by their covers and regretted it. In distributing this novel on an honesty basis, I hope to encourage you to try something new by shifting the risk away from you and on to me. Please read Dreamwords Book One and then pass it to another reader when you've finished – pointing to the honesty clause in the following page as you do.

If you think the next book should be published - and only then - please pay for this one. If you think otherwise or find that time to read eludes you, I release you from the bond and ask only that you pass it to a reader who agrees to the conditions set here. My aim is to find my future readers, to introduce them to Dreamwords and to give you the choice of deciding for yourself by voting with your money.

I have no trust fund or stash of cash. This is it. Dreamwords will live or die by what you do next.

Paul

This copy of Dreamwords Book One is £3.50 per reader (and your promise to pass the book on to the next person who agrees to the honesty deal). If you wish to own this edition - and thus take it out of circulation - it is £7.99.

To pay from the UK, text DREAMWORDS to 81456. The message will cost £3.50 plus a standard text at your network rate – a one-time charge. That's it.

To pay £7.99, please send a cheque or postal-order, crossed and made payable to me, at:

Paul Story

Unit 115,

111 West George Street,

Glasgow, G2 1QX, Scotland

If you are paying for the complete copy by post and include your postal or e-mail address with the cheque, I will inform you when the next in the series is published. Should I decide to repeat the format of this experiment, I will send you a copy of Book Two on a similar basis with no effort to chase payment beyond the measure of honesty you have already demonstrated.

Your details are confidential. They will not be passed to a third party and will be used solely for the purpose stated here.

For more information or to pay on-line, please visit:

www.dreamwords.com

About Paul Story:

Several years ago, I quit my job, dumped most of my possessions and simplified my life to two small bags and a rucksack. Since then, I have been fortunate in meeting many wonderful people, enjoyed the hospitality and generosity of strangers and attracted a modest fan-base for my work. For up to seven months in a year, I write from my tent in the Highlands - immersing myself in the world I am creating. This is my office, my home and my writing adventure. We hear that technology allows us to work from anywhere we like. From my thoughts to yours across the planet, from my fabric walls, through space and air and silicon and finally to paper, I know that this is true. If I can make it happen, anyone can. If I can work my way back to a normal life and yet remain in control of it, I will have lived the dream. For now, the cliff is there and the bottom is a long way down.

When I tell friends and family how I intend to launch Dreamwords many are appalled. I understand why and admit to the extreme risk I'm taking. Each person tells me that they wouldn't steal the book but that too many others will. Perhaps they are right, perhaps not.

We are conditioned by insurance companies, by politicians and by the constant barrage of horror stories in the media, to live in fear of bad things happening. While I do not suggest that shops ignore security or that you leave your car or house unlocked and unattended, I do feel that the balance of fear is wrong. In rightly protecting ourselves from thieves and other predators, we sometimes isolate ourselves from each other. I believe that people are generally good. Beyond the basics of survival, most are honest and will act accordingly given the chance.

I am about to show the world the truth of it - starting in Scotland - or to demonstrate that I am wrong. For every book that lands in the hands of an honest and satisfied reader, I will take a small step forward. For every book that lands in the hands of an honest reader who does not respond to the story, a happy reader is a short transfer away.

Enough honest people and The Dreamwords Series will live.

For Stephen

ONE

The boy opened his eyes to a blue sky. He lay on his back and, without moving his body, scanned what he could of his surroundings. He recognised nothing.

The soaring cliff above his head, the mossy vegetation he lay on, the wild green landscape rolling from his feet to the white-flecked sea were all strangers to him. The biggest stranger however, was the boy himself. He had no idea who or where he was.

His left leg was bent and tucked under his right knee. He sat up and slowly untangled himself, all the while expecting to reel back in pain from some debilitating wound. When at last he stood, the boy noted that the only signs of injury were a painfully bruised ankle, a vague headache, a cut on his left shoulder and his right hand covered in blood. The blood was dry and there was no obvious wound to produce such a mess. Perhaps the damage belonged to his shoulder. It was difficult to see. There was a redness there but not much. Maybe it had bled and had now stopped.

He hopped to a small rock, sat down and looked around at the grassy mountains behind him and the stretch of water to his front. A strong breeze cooled the sunny day. There were no clouds apart from a few high wispy streaks that might have been wind-blown aircraft trails.

He closed his eyes and tried to remember. His mind was not blank. Far from it. But the thoughts and images were cluttered, a confusion of random parts that could have been imagination. He opened his eyes again and returned to his immediate plight. He guessed that the mountain sheltered him from much of the wind because, out there, the water bucked its roughened surface from a base of dark blue to brilliant white tops that sprayed a sideways and dazzling horizontal rain. It was beautiful, but the boy was in no mood to enjoy it. He had to get help.

Testing his ankle, he limped to his feet and searched the area for signs of life. To his left and right, the shoreline stretched as far as he could see and the only creatures were seagulls, riding the windy gusts and swirls with screeching cries that barely made it to his ears.

Hobbling forward, he pushed through wild bracken and, although he was barely three hundred metres from the shore, it was an exhausting and painful half hour before he stumbled on a small path that hugged the coast.

He sank onto a patch of grass, untied his lace, and winced at the blackened skin under his left sock. He thought better of removing his footwear, worried that the obvious swelling might become so bad that he would not be able to get the thing back on.

He had no watch, but the sun was already sinking behind the mountain, casting a long and growing shadow that crept towards him like a black wave. It felt like spring or summer, so he guessed the time at somewhere between four and seven pm.

He retied the lace as loosely as he could and stood again. Turning left and right, he yelled, 'Hello!' There was no answer. Closer to the shore, the wind, although still unpredictable, was predominantly left to right and so, with the sea to his left, he turned the wind on his back and let it blow him along the well-worn path, towards an unknown destination.

*

Darkness eased onto the shadowed landscape. The cloudless sky dimmed to a deep blue that matched his bruise and then faded to black. A sliver moon was useless and the stars, although spectacular, did nothing to light his stumbling way.

After what seemed like hours, the ground became flat and the boy gentled himself to a smooth rock that ramped into the sea. Relieved of the pressure on his ankle, exhaustion closed him down. Sleep dragged his head to the stone pillow, eyelids closed by themselves and the tiny figure curled his knees to his chin and hugged his lonely body to oblivion.

*

The noise probably saved his life. It came from close by; a low animal grunt that, even to the most unimaginative, sounded like the throaty growl of a werewolf.

He leapt to his feet, his ankle forgotten. The night bound him like a shroud of black ice. Seawater slapped on rock and spat salt rain into the air, plastering the boy's clothes to his skin. He held his breath and listened.

The wind now blew onshore and steady. It, and the noisy sea at his back, made it difficult to hear, but a primal fear forced him to stand his ground until he located the noise.

Somewhere ahead, on the hill, the grumbling bark rose above the wind and surf. He drew a freezing breath of air and turned to face the sound. Indistinct shapes oozed through the darkness. The black mass of the hill was clear and, within its bulk, isolated trees and rocks gave shape to the void they shared.

A single gust of wind slammed from the right, forcing him to spread his feet and look to his balance. In that swift movement, in the action of looking away, he saw something from the corner of his eye - the vague notion of an animal, a dim blur that suddenly did not look so threatening. There was more than one of them and the boy realised that, what he thought was stalking him, was in fact a massive, but probably harmless, deer. And as quickly as the fear had gripped him, it was gone. Reabsorbed by the night, the herd dimmed; the threat all in his mind.

With this realisation, once adrenalin stopped pumping through his blood, the shaking started. Legs buckled and he tumbled back to his unsuitable bed.

Lying there, he knew that if he stayed he would die before the night was over. Wet and exposed to the wind, sea-spray hosed him in a fine mist more deadly than the apparent danger that had woken him. Teeth chattering, he almost cried at the unfairness of it all. *Why couldn't he just lie and sleep? It would be so easy.*

So final.

Miraculously, the cold seemed to disappear and a warm haze smothered his thinking.

On the hill, the deer barked another warning and the boy dragged himself back to discomfort. He had to get out of the wind. Climbing to his knees, he stumbled and crawled towards a large jumble of rocks. An automaton with no apparent plan, somehow he found what he was looking for and soon he was in the hole as though that had been his destination all along. Ten-ton bricks, jumbled in heaps, formed dozens of these mini-caves; a haven for animals and now the boy. The rock drew him in and the wind became background noise and nothing more. The false heat was gone too and he continued to shake. Out of the wind, he'd taken away the biggest danger, but it was already too late. He was so cold that unless he could warm himself, he would have been as well staying outside to let the false heat take him. Exposure and death stalked him to the hole.

And the stench!

Something smelled terrible. And when his hand fell on a mess of bone and flesh, he knew by the touch of clotted wool that it was the remains of a dead sheep.

Without realising it, the boy had already given in to the forces shutting him down. He lay with a stone the size of a hedgehog pressed to the small of his back. But somewhere beyond the weakness of his body another part of him fought on. This entity - the spirit hiding inside the boy's head - lifted his arm and grappled for the grizzly remains at his side, tugged a corner of skin that had been ripped by scavenging teeth and pulled. The carcass split and the coat and ribcage slid over him. The wool was close to his chest and the bones stuck upwards as though he'd just turned himself inside out.

Like this, and still shaking uncontrollably, he slept.

*

Free from movement and conscious thought, the boy's mind exploded through a universe of images and misshapen facts. Sewn among the nonsense however, was a jumble of coherent pictures and thoughts that could have been real or fabricated memories. There were faces and names, places and feelings, and all of them came and went in a blur.

At one point the sun penetrated his burrow in a small shaft of brilliant light that lit the twinned faces of the sheep and the boy. A girl, somewhere in the real world, shouted, 'I'm here!'

She was close, the quality of her voice different to those in his head. He strained through slitted eyes. A shadow flicked over the space above as a figure jumped from rock to rock. Still shivering, the weight on his eyelids irresistible.

He closed them and strained his lips to speak, but nothing came. He would have to move. Help was close. He would have to move or die.

Soon.

In a minute.

Move or die.

He counted to ten and then, with the will of a thousand saints, looked out at the world and saw that somehow those ten seconds had expanded to hours and it was dark again.

Disoriented, he struggled to his knees and circled the pit until he found the hole he'd entered by. Outside, a light drizzle pattered the ground and he contemplated returning to the relative warmth of his dead friend. But for how long would he be warm? Soon the rain would soak even that stinking haven. The effort to move had been so great that giving up this easily would be a cowardice that would surely kill him.

Thankfully, the apparition that was the girl had been moving in the same direction as he had the previous day. Forced to retrace his steps, the hollow tomb would have seemed so much brighter.

Stumbling and fumbling for the path, he was soon soaked from above and slicked in sweat. Drizzle became rain and rain became a torrent that fed numerous streams running down the mountain, crossing his path to the sea. To his left the breaking surf rolled pebble and sand; a steady rhythm of inhaled and exhaled breath. His hair, dirty and lank, dripped a small waterfall from his fringe so that he was forever wiping his face with one hand and then another.

This concert of water coalesced to form a constant hiss that felt as though his mind was not quite tuned in. Keeping to the path was at times impossible. It was clear enough, and mostly followed the shore, but every now and then it meandered right, lost through a patch of trees or bracken and the boy found himself falling over rocks and wading through mud to keep the forward progress flowing.

And then he saw it.

A lonely light shimmered through the rain. It seemed to be moving, as though a lamp carried by another traveller caught in the wet wilderness. As he watched and wiped his eyes, the light steadied to match the drunken sway of his body as he tried to stay upright.

Frightened to admit to himself that he thought he was looking at a cottage, he bit his tongue, but soon gave into a hope that panicked him into running wildly through stream and thorn and rain until there could be no doubt.

He was saved.

A white cottage, ghostly bright among the drab wash of gloom, shone from behind the veil of rain. He faltered and then stood for several seconds watching the building, looking at the small white rectangle that was the window, hoping to see an angel who would save him from the hell he had woken to.

At last, as if roused from another dream, he ran forward and rapped on the green wooden door.

TWO

A dazzling slab of light fell through the open door and a girl, about his own height, stared at him in wide-eyed disbelief. Wisps of black hair frizzed from under a towel wrapping her head. She opened her mouth to speak, but as she did, a large man pounded a narrow hallway, grabbed her arm, swung her away and slammed the door in the boy's face.

Considering the situation, his condition and the bizarre thoughts he'd been having, he was numb to logic and chuckled softly, his legs buckled and he sat on the grass in front of the doorstep. Inside, voices, a man's in particular, battled, feet stormed stairs and doors shuddered with sudden violence through the watery hiss.

Slipping sideways, he saw the door reopen, tree-trunk legs bending at the knees, large hands scooping him from the sodden ground. And so, the boy entered the cottage.

*

Still shivering and dreaming crazy dreams, he lay on a soft mattress, his clothes cut from his body, replaced by warm and dry cleanliness - cocooned inside a sleeping bag.

How long he lay in that state he was not sure but, by the cycle of light and dark through a chink in the cloth-covered window, it was more than a single day. When his mind became clear enough to think, he was surprised to note that he had not been taken to hospital or airlifted by helicopter as some part of him knew might be normal. Neither had he seen the girl. Was she even real? Perhaps she was simply the imagined shape of his rescuer; his angel. A Cinderella enslaved by a mad hermit. Was that his fate too?

Every now and then, a bowl of soup or hot chocolate or over-sweet tea was forced down his throat, but even so, when he awoke, he was ravenous.

The room was spare, damp and dingy. Everything was wood. Old. The boy lay still and listened. There was movement downstairs, but no talking and no way of telling whether there was one, two or more occupants in the house. Of course, there had to be at least two. Crossing the wooden floorboards on bare feet, he pulled the side of the makeshift curtain clear of the window. The weather had not improved. Rain hammered the glass. The sea, no more than twenty metres away, was grey and restless. A small, unfenced lawn beyond the front door was a cultivated island among wild and unkempt vegetation. He could see no road. Perhaps it ran behind the cottage.

He was dressed in a dark blue tracksuit. It was warm, but the dampness of the house and the cold boards on his feet made him shiver just the same. He could not understand why, but there was something about the place that unsettled him. *This was his sanctuary*, he told himself. *He was with friends; they'd saved him.* Why then did he continue to shake? Was the damp really that bad?

Of course, he decided, he was being stupid. He recrossed the floor, took a deep breath, prepared to thank his rescuers for their kindness and pulled on the doorknob to leave the room.

But nothing happened beyond the hollow sound of rattling wood and metal. The door was locked.

Why would they lock the door? Was he a prisoner?

He tapped the wood with a bent knuckle and said, rather hoarsely, 'Hello? Is anyone there?'

There was no reply.

He tried again, this time with more force.

'Hello. Let me out!'

Immediately the noise downstairs turned to whispers and then to a scuttling movement as though he had just disturbed foraging rats. Eventually footsteps shook the stairs and a key squealed and grated in the rusty lock.

A man, giant by any standards, loomed over him, his unsmiling face shabby and unshaven, his wide shoulders barely slim enough to squeeze through the frame. The boy stepped back and sank onto the bed.

'You're awake.'

This self-evident remark was almost an accusation as though the boy had no right to be awake at all.

'Yes,' he replied, with equal redundancy.

'You'll be hungry.'

At these words, he dared be nothing else, remembered that he really was ravenous and nodded his head vigorously.

The man backed out the door, closed it and then, with an action more efficient than words, locked him in again.

Not quite believing what had just happened, the boy tried the handle, but it was true. He was trapped.

THREE

Thirty minutes later, the man-mountain returned with a tray that seemed small in his hands and then suddenly enormous when plonked on the boy's lap as he sat, quite still, on the bed.

'Thank you, but I need - '

The giant cut him off. 'You'll be leaving in twenty minutes.' He bent down and retrieved a pile of clothes from the floor outside the room and tossed them on the mattress beside him. 'Be ready.'

He turned to leave and then looked back again. 'Do you need anything else?' His voice had mellowed, his face softened, but still the sense of menace filled the room.

'I.. I need the toilet.'

'Under the bed,' he said with something that could have been a smile or a scowl. The door closed, locked and then the house shook as boots as big as boats pounded down the stairs.

Bemused by the strange encounter, the boy placed the tray on the floor and tried the door once more. Sure enough, it was locked.

He ducked to scan the floor under the bed and, with a look of utter dismay, retrieved a white and chipped metal pot that was obviously his toilet. He glanced at his tray and then the pot and groaned. He had no choice. He forced himself to use the horrible thing after isolating his meal on a vacant shelf of an old wardrobe, shutting the door and moving to the far end of the room to do his business.

Swapping the meal for the foul pot, he quarantined the object in the wardrobe, retook his position on the bed and gave in to his hunger.

The meal was plain, but it was also delicious and plentiful. Mashed potatoes, beef, herbs and spices all lumped together in a ball of mush may not have been his perfect choice in some previous life, but, since he had no idea what that might have been, he was overtaken with the need for fuel and shovelled the heaped contents into his mouth. Lifting the plate close to his lips, the boy spooned the contents with animal haste into his body.

A mug of sweet tea had cooled by the time he was ready for it and a sudden thirst overtook him half way through the meal so that he gulped the liquid down in a few seconds.

Finished, he lay back on the bed, unable to move, thinking about his predicament. The man had told him he was leaving, said he was to get ready. *What was he going to do? Throw him out?* Perhaps they were close to a village. That had to be it. He had walked a long way. Or at least it had seemed like it.

Suddenly excited, he grabbed the bundle and put on what had been his old clothes. They were torn and poorly washed but no longer smelled of dead sheep. An attempt had been made at sewing his fleecy top with white thread over dark fabric. Not very fashionable but dry and for that he was thankful.

His curiosity about his strange rescuers was quickly overcome by his need to leave the prison this surely was.

The door opened as he finished lacing his boot. He was about to jump to his feet when he remembered his ankle, pulled the sock down and searched for the bruise. There was none. He ignored the man's unspoken command to hurry. 'How long have I been here?' he asked.

'Two days. We need to move. There's a storm coming.'

Two days. His ankle had healed completely in such a short time. He was sure it must have been longer but, why would the man lie? There was no bruise, no swelling, and when he stood, there was no pain. He shrugged and followed the retreating figure downstairs towards a blustery and unbelievably wet day. There was so much he wanted to ask the giant. Where were they? What was the man's name? The girl's? But as he caught up with him on the doorstep, a waterproof jacket flew at him, wrapping itself around his head so that he nearly tripped in blind confusion over a scraggy piece of carpet.

'Put it on.'

Stepping into the open, he wrapped himself in the yellow-red jacket which fitted perfectly. He zipped it to his chin, his hair already dripping water, his trousers soaked all the way down the left side in a line that matched the direction of the wind. By the time he pulled the hood over his head, the man was hauling a small boat mounted on a rusting frame on wheels down a concrete ramp into the sea.

Seeing him struggle, the boy ran to help, but the boat was already there, the rolling surf floating and then grounding the thing in waves of easy violence. Without saying a word, an orange life-vest was pushed at him and he obediently put it on.

'Jump in,' the man ordered and stilled the bucking craft as best he could. Wading to his calves, water flooded his boots and froze his lower limbs. He grabbed the edge and timed his jump to the rhythm of the lurch, tumbling head-first into the fish-stinking slime at the bottom of the boat. The man followed with surprising grace. He took an oar and pushed down on the sea-bed until they were deep enough for the outboard motor to take over.

Pulling the toggle, the boy's rescuer started the engine first time and a second later they headed out to sea.

FOUR

To be in a small boat in such weather was crazy. The boy knew this instinctively but, at that moment, felt nothing but the urge to leave. They vectored right on a tip of land formed from the curving shore that enclosed them in a semi-bay. It was soon evident that the spit protected them from the worst of the sea because, as they rounded the headland, the water became a shifting tar of mountain and trough. It launched and dropped them with terrifying speed up one side of a wave and down the other. The boy sat at the front white-knuckling the wooden edges and staring down the abyss, while the man gripped the tiller at the stern, eyes unblinking, gazing ahead as though boating in a duck pond. Plunging down each sickening slope, it seemed as though the bow would cleave the surface and continue to the bottom of the ocean, but then they'd level out and climb back up the other side to repeat the drop to near certain death.

They travelled along the coastline, but had to go out to sea and then turn and come back again in a saw-tooth pattern to avoid being caught by a wave side-on. If that were to happen, the tiny boat would be swamped and tipped over. The boy checked the strap on his life-jacket for the tenth time. It was still secure. He checked it again.

Water sloshed under his feet from bow to stern, from port to starboard, carrying with it a mess of flotsam that included, greasy trousers, an old rope, a red fuel can and a jar of worms. With each plunge and spray the boat filled and gained weight, the sea crept higher and the craft sank lower.

They had just made a perilous turn back to the shore when the man looked behind him from the crest of a wave and cursed the blackening sky. The storm powered towards them.

Slamming the rudder hard, the man made his first sensible decision of the day. The dingy leaned dangerously to starboard, seemed to pause on the verge of a mountainous void and then swivelled, just in time, for the free-fall back the way they came.

Amidst the sound of water and wind, the pair remained resolute and silent. They had to get back. They should never have left the cottage in the first place.

*

The shore ahead was rocky, an unbroken line of white surf smashing itself to a fine mist, running from the headland they'd recently rounded and continuing left for the next three miles.

Fifty metres from the foaming rocks and the same to the tip of the apostrophe marking the edge of safety, the storm hit them.

They had been running swiftly, the wind blowing onshore, the tiny engine and the rudder carrying them easily towards their escape. When the storm attacked, the gale smacked them in the face, broiled the heaving sea, pushed them away from the calm water that seconds before seemed so close.

'Hang on!' the man screamed above the roar. Once again, he changed tack, this time pushing as close to the peninsula as he dared, hoping to skim it before the storm pushed them onto the rocks.

The boy gripped the sides, watching with grim fascination, as a bright yellow plastic crocodile, no more than five metres to his left, flew through the air on a foaming wave of white death and slid on the backwash to repeat the leap again and again. Slowly, slowly, the jut of land and the little toy eased behind them. Amid the thunder of the surf and the raging wind and rain, the scream of the outboard motor as it clawed the water, their pace against the land was almost serene. At last, as the crocodile broke in two, the pitiful craft entered what had been the relative calm, on a line towards the cottage. This did not, however, mean they were safe.

With the changing direction and sudden ferocity of the elements, the shelter of the peninsula was minimal.

When they at last saw the cottage, it was shrouded by a shifting veil of rain. Earlier, as they had left the building, the steady torrent slanted diagonally in regimented lines, now each droplet was a member of a swarm, sweeping down and then curving suddenly upwards and sideways in waves that seemed alive.

And then there was the girl - staggering along the shore close to the ramp, yelling silently as they struggled towards her. Even the man's voice barely reached him as he screamed himself hoarse. 'Inside. Get in. Inside now!'

A strong gust pushed them sideways and the boat skewed to port, sliding in dreamlike slow motion over the crest of a black hill, the wind changing so that they were held aloft, it seemed, by opposing forces.

And then it died. Just like that. It was only for a couple of seconds. It died or changed direction, the effect was the same. They hurtled forward and down, the bow slamming hard into the trough, the wooden prow submerging like a submarine on a crash dive. As they hit, the boy pitched forward and involuntarily closed his eyes - and as he did that, he suddenly pictured his own back, as though from inside the head of the man behind him. A hairy hand reached out, intent it seemed to push him hard between the shoulders. He saw himself lurch over the bow and into the churning sea.

The episode, or vision, had flashed through his mind, literally, in a blink. It was so fast that he had no time to think about what it was he actually saw. Instead, his natural instinct to survive kicked in and he tried to escape the murdering act. He leant forward as they hit the bottom. The wave washed over them, the boat juddered to a slow crash and everything; the old trousers, the petrol can, the rope, the sloshing bilge and the boy himself catapulted down. The boy turned instinctively and saw the hand, the man's face contorted by exertion, stretching for his back and all at once he lost his grip and slipped over the transom to be swallowed by the furious sea.

FIVE

In his first second underwater, the world calmed to a surreal dream of embryonic comfort. The wind, the rain, the bucking boat, the fight, the numbness of his hands, the white knuckles, the terror of falling in, were all gone; replaced in that beat by a fluid that at first seemed warm, and the pounding in his ears a mother's heart.

And then he surfaced and entered Hell all over again.

The boat reared over him like a wild horse, its rider leaning out and down to run him under. The boy turned away, kicked out at the hull, tried to dive, but his life-jacket wouldn't let him. The giant hand snapped forward and grabbed his foot, the foot kicked and sausage fingers smashed against the boat and let go.

If the man fell overboard or dived in after him, the boy wasn't sure, but suddenly he was there, arms pinning his, their combined weight dragging them down, the girl on the shore bobbing in and out of sight, screaming - wind and tide driving them towards a small clump of rocks. A breath, the gurgle of submerged surf, the death and rebirth of the storm, choking on salt lungs, a half-breath, arms limp, rocks close, the land thrown at them, and underwater a sudden crack of bone, a scream and the boy crawled up the pebbled beach as the girl dived to save the broken man, battling his pain on the edge of death.

Exhausted and confused, the boy hauled himself to his feet and turned back to face the sea. There he saw the girl, her sodden blue jeans and pink jersey out of kilter with her elemental struggle for life. She had the man's arm, but instead of pulling him to shore, a giant wave lifted them both from their feet, and on the outflow, carried them further out to sea. To the left, the boat and the rock, closing, the snap of wood, the scream of metal on stone as the propeller spun to destruction. A brief smell of ozone.

Something drew his attention to the water between his position on the beach and the struggling figures. It was the red petrol can and beside it the rope from the bottom of the boat, half submerged and likely to disappear at any moment.

Powered by pure adrenalin, he staggered to the water and grabbed a loop before the storm could steal it away. In two seconds flat, he had tied a bowline as expertly as any climber and tossed it to the girl. The wind spat it back and another wave washed the pair towards him once more. Recovering quickly, he tried again. They were only twenty feet away, but in the fury of the storm it could have been a hundred. The rope spun once over his head and flew on a lucky gust. The girl sprung from the water like a porpoise, thrust a hand through the falling loop and hooked it in the crook of her arm.

Pulling them to the beach was easy. Then, repositioning the rope under the man's arms, the girl and the boy heaved him in concert with the waves up to the top of the shore, no more than forty feet from the cottage door.

The rock around them ran red. It looked as though a fountain of blood had gushed from the man's arteries, spreading his life in a thin smear on the lonely shore. In fact, all they could find was a small cut on his forehead and, messy as it was, their immediate concern was to get out of the storm. His right leg looked strange and the boy remembered the underwater crack and winced as he recalled the sound of the man's breaking bone. He seemed unconscious, but when another wave re-floated him and dragged his injured limb over the pebbles, he lurched upright, grasped the leg with both hands and bellowed like a bull on a sword.

This cry of anguish galvanised the girl. 'Help me!' she yelled. Together, the man trailing his broken leg, the girl to his right, the boy his left, they staggered from the storm, to the warmth and safety of the desolate, and isolated, white cottage.

SIX

Katriana was her name. His Angel.

She moved quickly, with the confidence of a general. If she had let him, the boy could easily have collapsed in an exhausted bag of bones as soon as the door slammed behind them, but her brisk efficiency and her courage infected him like a drug. For some reason he did not want to seem weak in her presence and, perhaps for the sake of that same reason, was keen to follow her orders.

They placed the injured man on a settee at the back of the house on the ground floor and as Katriana removed the life-jacket, the waterproofs and cut the trousers from his bad leg, she told the boy to light a fire.

'The cold will kill him, not the leg,' she said.

By the time the fire raged in the grate, the man was down to a pair of white Daffy Duck boxers and the girl rubbed him furiously with an enormous tartan towel. He tried to speak, but every time his mouth opened, the pain flew from his body in a plaintiff groan that would terrify a ghost.

'Sshhh,' she whispered. 'Save your strength.' And then to the boy she barked. 'The kitchen. Boil some water. Hot drinks.'

By the time he did so and returned with three mugs of sweet tea, she had somehow managed to dress the giant in a dry fleece and woollen long-johns and got him into a bed in the far corner of the room.

The boy handed her a tea. She looked at the steam rising from the brown liquid, brought her face close to the rim and pulled back sharply. 'It's too hot.'

He obediently retreated to the kitchen, ran some cold water into the mugs and returned to her side. She held the warm drink to the man's chattering lips and nodded her approval as he gulped the heat back into his body.

Next, she pushed back a corner of the duvet and examined his leg, all the time whispering in a manner that the boy thought was meant to exclude him. Was she keeping him busy to keep him away? When he tried to give the girl a mug of her own she nodded towards a table and he dutifully placed it there. He was about to ask if he could help when she spoke with abrupt efficiency.

'Through the front room. The drawers on the right, you'll find a dry set of clothes. Take what you need.'

'What about - ?' He was going to ask her about herself; she was as wet as he was - her long hair separating to dripping strands of liquorice - but she cut him off. 'Just do it!' And then she softened. 'I'll be fine. Dry yourself and change.'

The boy once more did as he was told. He found the drawers and, peeling himself layer by layer, he realised how right the girl had been. With her tacit permission, he collapsed inwardly, taking a full five minutes to remove the trousers that seemed to have fused with his skin. When at last he'd changed, he lay on the floor by the wet pile of clothes, fell asleep and dreamt.

*

The dream was fragmented, the editor in his head jumping from scene to scene in search of cohesion.

He was in a car, a bald man driving. The driver wiry, with a smile that slid around his face to grin at the boy from his left cheek, while his head remained motionless to the front.

Keep your eyes on the road.

Headlights dazzled them. A curse from the driver. The boy's hand on the door. The door opens. Screeching tyres. And then a tree. The door wrenched from his hand. Flying and rolling and then running through the night.

And soon he stood on a cliff top. The driver, his mouth back in place, the grin just as ugly.

The mouth spoke. Its head a pale moon. The words oozed like puss from his lips, floated across the night and circled the boy's mind.

'Corven, Corven, Corven.'

And then they stood together, a rock in the boy's hand. He

swung it hard. The arc ended on the pale moon and the pale moon crumpled over the cliff and the boy dropped the rock and stared at his bloodied right hand.

*

When he awoke, he was wrapped in a blanket, lying on an old sofa, his legs overlapping the curved arm at the far end, his head cradled by the softest pillow in the universe. A fire crackled behind the safety of a wire guard, the direct heat on his face infusing his body and for the first time since he could remember, which admittedly wasn't long, he felt happy to be where he was.

To his left, Katriana huddled under a blanket too, her feet tucked up on the musty armchair, her covered knees touching her chin, her hair brushed, dry and shiny again. Slowly, he turned his head to look around, trying at the same time not to waken her. They were in a room he did not recognise. There was no curtained bed, no chest of drawers. He could not recall getting there, nor the lighting of the fire. Although there was still a sense of disuse about the cottage, with two fires on the go, the warm blanket and the girl close by, the place, at that moment, was a cosy shelter from the storm that still raged outside.

He was settling back to think about his situation, trying to make sense of his fragmented thoughts, when he realised that the girl's eyes were open and she was staring at him. He attempted a smile and suddenly felt awkward.

'How did I - ?'

'You were cluttering the scullery. Very untidy.'

They were silent for a while, the sound of crackling wood, the hypnotic effect of flame and heat, the storm shaking the cottage with each sudden gust.

When she finally broke the spell, her words, innocently spoken, burrowed so deeply into his subconscious that he knew they held a fundamental truth that lay at the centre of who he was.

'You spoke in your sleep. Your name. Is it Tom Corven?'

And it fit him perfectly. It felt right. Something profound lay at the heart of those words. He knew his name.

Tom Corven.

He smiled at her. 'I think so. Yes. Tom Corven.'

But with the acceptance of his name came the memory of his

dream and he thought of the blood on his hand when he first awoke at the base of the cliff. He remembered the rock, the brief jolt of the man's skull and then the give as the weapon penetrated soft tissue. And the bald man crumpled over the cliff and died.

He was Tom Corven indeed. Tom Corven, the murderer.

SEVEN

Without a name, the boy had felt like a non-person. He craved a label as though it held his soul. He felt like a good person and a good person would have a good name. But Tom Corven was tainted, the soul corrupt, the label a stain on his developing self-image.

He couldn't take the name without the guilt. A part of him denied the charge. Surely he would know if he was a murderer. He would feel the evil inside. And because he didn't, he reasoned, the dream was just a dream.

He wrestled with his conscience, trying to master his thoughts before he engaged with Katriana, before he brought her to the shame of his deed.

His instinct was to push the conclusion away. But that was too easy. The blood on his hand was real enough. It was gone when he awoke in the cottage but that wasn't surprising. If his night in the rain hadn't washed it off, then his rescuers would have when they cleaned him up. Did they see the blood? Perhaps that was why they had acted so strangely towards him. He was now sure that the incident on the boat was a mixture of dé-jà vu and imagination. Far from attempting to kill him, the man had tried to stop Tom from toppling from the boat and saved him when he did.

His rescuers were suspicious of him. From the moment he'd arrived, they'd kept him at a distance. And who could blame them? He was suspicious of himself.

But what now?

If he had killed someone, even in self defence, the police would be after him; the very people he'd run to when he reached civilisation would be as likely to arrest as help him. A criminal - a murderer - might feign amnesia to escape punishment. Perhaps that's what he would be accused of. He really knew who he was, but pretended otherwise.

And who was the driver? The bald man. His victim.

The questions curdled and spun in his head, the conclusions buried, distant and deep.

He distilled what he thought he knew.

The deep-rooted belief that he was Tom Corven would not disappear and so, Tom Corven he was. The blood on his hand was real. It was his right hand, the same one that held the rock. He'd woken, injured, at the base of a cliff in the middle of nowhere. Perhaps the very cliff where he'd killed the bald man.

A deep groan rumbled the air like whispering thunder, the distant sound of pain in the next room an echo of the boy's violent past.

With no memory of the event beyond the brief and disjointed scenes in his dream, Tom tried to feel what he had felt then.

In the car. Edged to the door, one hand poised, ready to strike and the other on the handle. His heart pumping liquid fear through his veins.

He was being kidnapped. No-one would blame him. It was surely self-defence.

He would go to the police.

The alternative was to go on the run, not knowing who he was, where he came from and whether he was a killer, or the winner in a battle for life. The cottage shook, the blackness of the night a dark patch of rectangular glass on the wall. Tomorrow, he decided. He would find his way out tomorrow and hand himself in.

That settled, Tom looked at the dying fire. He eased himself from the sofa, removed the guard and placed a solid log onto the glowing ashes from a small pile by the side of the hearth.

'Open the vent at the bottom.'

Tom looked up, mildly startled by the intrusion.

Katriana's dark eyes reflected the soft glow of burning embers.

'It needs oxygen.'

Tom nudged the hot vent with a piece of kindling and the embers brightened as a small yellow flame licked the edge of the log and danced for their pleasure.

Replacing the guard, he returned to the sofa, took the duvet and curled up to face the girl.

'Your father. How is he?'

The girl blushed or the catching fire reddened her cheeks. She considered his question for so long that he wondered if she had not heard him. When he was about to repeat himself, she said. 'He's not my father.'

Tom didn't know what to say to that. He was so caught up in his own problems that he gave little thought to the relationship between the girl and the man.

'Sorry,' he said. 'I just thought - '

'He.. He's my uncle.'

Her confidence had disappeared. She was now a little girl, stammering replies that sounded like lies. Why she would lie was a mystery, but that was what it sounded like. He let it pass. Her reasons were none of his concern.

'How is he? Eh... you're uncle.'

'I'm worried. I've made a splint, but he needs a doctor.'

'Don't you have a phone?'

'No phone, no car, no road. We're four miles from the nearest village at Lochranza.'

Lochranza. He had heard the name before but could not place it.

'Where are we? This place?'

She looked at him curiously. 'Creggan Cottage,' she said.

He raised his eyebrows and she continued.

'You really don't know, do you?'

'I can't remember a thing. I woke up a few miles from here and before now didn't even know my name.'

'That's so weird.'

'How was I when I got here?' He wanted to ask her about the blood, but dreaded her answer.

'Like death. You babbled. Rubbish mostly. But you're strong. By rights you should be on your back still.'

He remembered how quickly his leg had healed and mentioned this to her.

'Your ankle was fine, Tom. Not a mark on you.'

He must have misheard her, he was thinking, but she sat up, her eyes frowning with concern. 'There was nothing wrong with you except for a few maggots in your hair. And your hand. You were obsessed with your hand.'

Tom held his breath. Whether he liked it or not, the answer he needed to hear was coming his way. Was he evil or simply mad?

She lowered her voice. 'You wanted us to wash it clean. Kept screaming about the blood.' She glanced at his hand then and averted her gaze when she saw that he had noticed. 'There wasn't a mark on you, Tom. No blood, no cut. Nothing.'

*

So there it was. He was mad. He had been convinced that something evil lay at Tom Corven's core and with Katriana's words, he should have been comforted. If it had been a simple matter of his non-stained hand, he could assume that the rain had washed him clean, but there was more. Initially relieved, Tom was puzzled when Katriana explained that she had meant what she said about him being free from injury. According to the girl, his ankle and shoulder were as spotless as his hand and so his descent to madness continued. If he could not rely on the recall of his journey to the cottage, how could he give credence to the fantasy of his dreams?

Yes, Katriana's words should have brought him comfort, but they did not. How could he explain himself? Why was he obsessed with his hand? Why did he wipe it and wipe it and wipe it?

Whoever the old Tom was, the new one, the one sitting with Katriana in a remote cottage, the one trying to make sense of himself - *this Tom* - did not like lying.

But the alternative was so awful - too messy to try to explain, too complicated. Too shameful. Soon he'd be out of Katriana's life. For now he would settle for the simplicity of selective truth.

'I used a dead animal to keep warm,' he told her, 'I felt dirty.'

'And I thought you might have been raised on a maggot farm,' the girl quipped.

Tom shivered. 'I'll go for help tomorrow,' he said, determined to change the subject.

She gestured to the window. 'I doubt it. This could last for days.'

'Great!' Tom looked disappointed, but really warmed to the thought of Katriana's company and stealing time to rebuild his sanity.

'Tell me. I know we're in Creggan Cottage but where exactly is that?'

'I take it you know we're on planet Earth,' she smiled.

'Let's start from there. What country?'

'Scotland.'

As soon as she said it, Tom knew that it was right. The feeling was akin to the recognition of his name. And now that he knew, it felt as though he'd always known, although the sense could have been an illusion.

'Close to Lochranza,' he offered.

'Right. Arran, South West of Glasgow.'

There it was again. Recognition without triggering anything new.

She continued. 'You have a Scottish accent.'

'I do?' This was a revelation. He could hear Katriana's accent and that of her uncle's, but when he listened to his own voice, to his ear, there was no hint of a dialect.

They talked, the conversation frequently punctuated by Katriana checking on the man next door. Tom tried to find out more about the girl but she appeared reluctant – evasive even. Instead, she spoke of her love for the Island, how she and her parents used to come here when she was little and how her father had taken her on his shoulders to the summit of Goat Fell when she was only four.

'My mother was furious when she found out. We were supposed to be walking around Brodick Castle, later perhaps, an easy stroll up the path a little. But, apparently I pointed to the top and said 'Daddy. Go there. Up there.'

Those dark drowning-pool eyes held him as she told the story. She seemed to remember something sad and fell to silence for a few seconds before suddenly brightening again. 'Tea,' she said.

Tom jumped to his feet to beat her to it, but she did the same and they both overbalanced and collapsed back onto their seats. 'Tea,' they chorused.

'Stay where you are. You need to rest.' The general was back. Tom accepted defeat and Katriana drifted to the kitchen to boil the kettle.

Unable to settle, he got up, put another log on the fire and wandered the room. There was no electricity in the cottage, the moody light of the fire bolstered by a portable gas lamp that hissed constantly in the background. There were paintings on the wall, old and faded; all showing various scenes on the island and all, he guessed, impersonal to the occupants. They were stained; a yellowing state of decay. The more he looked, the more curious he became. He'd assumed that Katriana lived here at first and then doubted that as he took in its remote situation and the dampness pervading the building. Now he realised that it was more fundamental than that. If this was a retreat, then he would have expected to see some personal artefacts; photographs, paintings and even some of the comforts of home. Creggan Cottage was more like a seldom visited museum, full of the history of dead people. Even if they'd rented it, he would have expected the same attention to detail from its owner.

He moved to a window and cupped his hand over the glass to exclude the reflection from the room. He was at the back of the house but could see nothing but rain weeping across the pane. Returning to the fire, Tom noted that the second log had not caught. He removed the fire-guard to attend to it, but as he bent his head to the vent, a sudden down-draft swept the chimney, carrying with it a choking fog of smoke and ashes that blackened the boy in dust and fumes. He reeled back, gasping in fright and felt Katriana's hand on his shoulder.

'Careful,' the voice said.

Spluttering and wiping tears from his eyes, he spun to the girl, explaining, 'It's the storm, it blew – '

But he was quite alone. There was no Katriana, no-one chiding his carelessness. He whispered in sudden fear, invisible cockroaches crawling over his neck. 'Hello? .... Hello?' Tom could see he was alone but that made no sense. 'Who's there?'

Something small scurried behind the skirting boards. A fly, suddenly noisy, buzzed the dead air.

Outside, the elements battled and a gentle clink of china drifted from the kitchen, accompanied by a groan of stifled agony; Katriana's uncle, dead to the world in the next room.

EIGHT

When Katriana entered a few seconds later, Tom was still blinking tears from his stinging eyes. He remained with his back to the fire staring at the spot where the person had to have stood to tap him on the shoulder. If he had been thinking logically, he might have shrugged the incident off as a trick of his disturbed mind, but the experience reawakened his sense of unease about the place, the feeling that something lurked in the shadows. Waiting.

When the girl saw the ashen face and ash tears, she placed the two mugs she was carrying on the mantelpiece and took him gently by the shoulders. 'Tom? What is it?'

When he didn't answer, she looked around the room, trying to figure out what he was staring at.

Tom suddenly realised that he was no longer alone. He focused on Katriana and the cottage became the warm, dry shelter it had been before she left the room.

'The fire. A draft, I think.'

'Sit down,' she commanded.

He sat, mesmerized by her gently swaying hair, its black sheen reflecting the suddenly healthy fire.

'Drink this. You're still weak'

He was about to agree with her when the thought of continued lies unsettled him. 'I saw something. No. I felt - *heard* - something.'

Katriana sat facing the boy on the sofa, her legs tucked under her. Tom sat straight, as though his spine had petrified.

'It's...' Katriana paused, changing her words mid-flow. 'My uncle.'

Tom realised that she was talking about the man in the next room.

'I gave him a half bottle of whisky. He's blowing his own hurricane.'

She was humouring him.

'No. It wasn't that. It was a woman.' He looked at the fire as though expecting to see her face in the flames. 'She spoke to me.'

Katriana felt his forehead and eased him back onto the pillow. He hadn't thought about her reaction. Perhaps she saw his madness. 'You're confused,' she told him, and of course, that was true. But she did not ridicule the intensity of his experience. She re-spread the blanket, placed a cushion at the other end of the sofa and tucked herself in so that they could talk facing each other without the cricked necks they'd endured earlier.

'Was she young or old?'

'Young. I think.'

'You didn't see her?'

'She was behind me. When I turned, there was no-one.'

They sat drinking from the steaming mugs; steaming still, because, despite the direct warmth of the fire on their faces, there was an all pervading chill to the air. It reminded him of the night he'd spent freezing and wet by the sea and then in his cave.

Katriana put her mug to her lap and looked directly at the boy. 'Do you believe in ghosts, Tom?'

It was a simple question, but to Tom, a response that required self knowledge was anything but simple.

'I don't know.' This was literally true. He didn't know what he believed.

'There has to be something.' Katriana said. It seemed as though she would expand on this, but the thought froze on her lips for a moment before finding the words she needed. 'I mean, there has to be something - when we die. Our souls. Heaven.'

'Hell.'

'Yes,' she said. 'I suppose that too.'

'This place.' He looked about the room, dark shadows writhing in the corners. 'What's its history?'

'Don't know.' She was going to leave it there, but noted Tom's puzzled expression and elaborated. 'It's not ours. We borrowed it from a friend. We've never been here before.'

This answered some of his questions, but there was still something missing. He couldn't place it, so he continued to probe blindly. 'It's a bit desolate for a holiday getaway.'

She shivered, the boy's mood infusing her with a sense of foreboding. She shook herself and forced a smile. 'It's not always like this. It's really beautiful. Peaceful like. Sometimes, it's even busy. Weekends there's a procession of walkers. Children, dogs.'

He smiled at this thought, the notion that they would not be isolated forever briefly comforting. 'Everything but door-to-door salesmen,' he said.

Katriana giggled and a tiny splash of tea escaped her mug. 'They used to make millstones cut from a quarry close by. There's still a huge rock-wheel a half mile along the shore. It weighs tons. All that work and they just abandoned it.'

'And now they're dead.'

Tom tried to imagine the people who lived in the cottage then. It looked old, but in truth, he had no idea of the time-scales involved. The notion gave life to the old place and he fantasized that it had once been home to children, growing in the folds of the cruel beauty of nature.

'I had an aunt who swears she could talk to the dead.'

Tom leaned forward.

'She was a medium. Good, too. Apparently. People used to travel miles to see her. Told me I had an aura. The gift.'

'Have you tried it?'

'I've watched. Been in the circle, like. But never actually done it.'

Tom was about to suggest they have a go now. He was so tense from his experience and overdosed on mystery that the thought of doing nothing was impossible. Before he could ask her, however, she shivered and continued. 'I don't think I could ever do that. I mean, if they're real - ghosts that is - I don't want them crawling through walls and under my skin. If..'

But Tom had stopped listening, distracted by a sudden movement beyond the girl's shoulder. A figure drifted through the closed door - a young woman - she looked directly at Tom, her eyes wide, long pleated dress torn from foot to knee and mud streaked down the left half of her face and neck. She was breathless, glanced behind her, around the room and then at the boy.

'Tom,' she cried. 'Get out. Get out now before it's too late.'

NINE

Tom jumped to his feet and spoke with a rasping voice that seemed to come from someone else. 'Who are you?'

'Tom? What's up, Tom?' Katriana looked from the boy to the closed door and back again. When he did not move, she got up, grasped and shook his shoulders.

Tom stared past the girl at the figure behind her. The apparition opened her mouth and something incoherent drifted through Tom's consciousness. She repeated herself and this time the boy deciphered the words to something that almost made sense. 'Under the hag stone.'

As Tom watched with horrified fascination, the sound dried to silence, her lips still moving, Katriana's frenzied shaking, lost to the strange vision. Tom was transfixed. The woman lifted her left hand and fingered an object hanging from a string chain around her neck. Tom focused on her elegant fingers as they stroked the simple piece of jewellery. She turned her head to look behind her and returned to gaze at Tom and speak to him in utter silence. Tom's attention was drawn to the chain, to the caressing fingers, to the stone that lay beneath them. And that's what it was - a stone. A pebble, perhaps taken from the beach beyond the door, fashioned into a simple heart, smooth and simple and beautiful.

The apparition looked down at the pendant and then at the boy. They held each other's gaze for half a beat that stretched to hours. The moment was shattered by an explosion of sound and wood, the door splintering to small pieces that showered the room. The woman cowered and Tom flinched, staggering backwards. The shock of this broke the hypnotic grip and when Tom drew his eyes back to the woman, she was gone, the door untouched and still closed.

Tom wrenched himself from Katriana's grip. He pushed past her, threw open the door and staggered into the hallway. 'Who are you? What do you want from me?' But his words echoed in the empty hallway.

Running from room to room, from shadow to shadow, he searched in vain for the woman, ignoring the girl at his back trying to calm him and the nagging certainty that he would find nothing. When Katriana barred the door to the injured man's room, she hissed her frustration. 'Calm down, Tom. If you wake him...' She nodded behind her. ' He's in so much pain. It's cruel.'

But Tom pushed past her again, his livid skin bloodened by the red cast of the fire. The man snored like a cartoon giant and, satisfied that there was no-one else lurking within, Tom left and pounded the stairs.

Katriana waited in the hallway, listening to the drumming feet, wincing at the slamming doors. When he returned a minute later, it was not to the warmth of the blanket and the fire but to the wild fury they'd so recently escaped. He ran into the night storm like a madman searching for a stolen moon.

Katriana stood in the doorway, flurries of water blasting and retreating from her body. 'Tom,' she yelled again. The boy stood, drenched, framed by the light from the hallway, his back to the cottage, looking out to sea as if he could see into the featureless pitch of night.

His shoulders slumped, the energy of moments before gone. He turned slowly, walked back inside and Katriana closed the door. 'We'll get you dry,' she said quietly.

'There's something wrong with me.'

Katriana's frustration was tempered now by the helplessness in the boy's voice. He seemed so lost. So vulnerable.

'You've been through hell,' she said. 'It won't last forever.'

Later, when they were dry and back in the same positions on the sofa, the fire blazing healthily, a mug of soup cupped in each of their hands, Katriana broached the subject with analytical calm.

'You should talk about it.'

'There's nothing to talk about. I'm seeing things. I've lost my mind.' Tom actually smiled at this thought. It felt as if that was exactly what he'd done; misplaced his mind. His memories gone. Lost.

'Tell me what she looked like.'

Tom brought the woman to his thoughts with surprising clarity. As he did, the warmth of the fire seemed to fuse with an inner glow that radiated from the image he held in his mind and spread throughout his body. She was young, perhaps in her late twenties. Very beautiful, her clothing plain, her dress long and loose, giving her an air of purity. The heart-shaped jewellery. At that point, drawing on the memory of her standing there, she had long blonde hair piled high on her head. His own imagination seemed able to ply the image because the woman smiled, even though he had only seen her in distress. She was speaking to him, a small laugh creasing the corners of her eyes. She wore no make-up but her skin shone its pale beauty, making her blue eyes dazzle.

Tom described what he saw as he focused on each aspect of the woman. What he didn't say was in the tone of his voice, the dreamy tilt of his head with each new discovery.

'And this is the woman who disturbed you so?' Katriana was right. Gone was the spectral horror in front of him, gone was the fright of the explosion and gone too was the sense of helplessness he had felt only minutes before. It was as though part of him had formed a favourable opinion of the woman that relied on information beyond his current grasp.

The girl had finished her drink and was now curled on the other side of the sofa, the cover up to her chin. Her voice was as sleepy as Tom felt. He nodded at her observation of his changed mood. 'The shock of seeing her I suppose. It's different now. I'm.....,' he paused in thought. 'Curious,' he said.

'But she's not real.'

Tom snuggled into the cushion at his head and held the woman's image in his mind. He knew that they should move, get to where they could spread out, but still he melted into the sofa, the sanctuary of Katriana's company and the inner warmth flowing from the strange intoxicating woman. The woman that common sense told him did not exist.

There was something else. As he lay there trying to pin down his feelings, feelings that had swung between fear and longing, between concern for his sanity and concern for Katriana and the non-existent ghosts; a subtle change settled on him. It crept up while he was thinking of concrete things and took him by stealth. When he recognised the change, it was already well established and difficult to shake. That night - a lifetime ago - when Tom had stumbled on the cottage, he thought he had done so by chance, but now he wasn't so sure. He still knew little of consequence about the place - he could not visualise what lay beyond the hill, had no idea what Lochranza might look like. What had changed was a recognition of something within himself. In some place, deep and inaccessible, a germ of familiarity struggled for growth. He couldn't put a face or an image to the feeling but it was so intense that he could not shake it from his mind. He had never seen Creggan Cottage before in his life, but that life was only a few days old. A small window opened on another existence. An old self. Another Tom.

And now he was certain:

He had been here before.

TEN

When Tom awoke, the dim light of day dulled the room, the fire a cold pile of grey ash that matched the sky beyond the window. The storm continued to shake the cottage. To the boy, it had raged unabated for most of his existence. He was stiff, his neck pushed up against the sofa's armrest, the cushion on the floor, his legs curled to his chest.

Katriana was gone. He slowly stretched to full length and listened. Her voice feathered through the walls as she talked to her uncle in the next room. There was no rumbling answer.

He was warm under the blanket and the damp air on his face caused him to huddle deeper beneath its cover. He thought about his situation. Despite his ordeal he was physically well. His ankle, his shoulder, his aching head had all recovered. He was hungry again but it was a healthy hunger, his body craving fuel for a life worth living.

He knew his name and felt a passionate longing to know more. He looked to the door and recalled the ghost with ease, as though she had reappeared at his bidding. This was a talent he began to recognise as a gift or a curse. His short-term memory and his imagination forged a cinematic Picasso; tantalising, disturbing, confused.

Once again he was able to alter the view he had of her. Her arms outstretched. Inviting an embrace, laughter-lines creased. Tom imagined himself enfolded by those arms and enjoyed the simple pleasure of the thought. A brief escape from isolation.

In the logic of daylight, he noted that the sense of familiarity he felt earlier was still there. So too was the yearning to recover something elusive. Its name, this elusive concept was beyond his grasp but somehow recognised by him as more precious than all his other memories combined.

He should have been desperate to leave Creggan Cottage, but he wasn't. True, his hosts were acting strange - there was something beyond the story they had fed him about an uncle and niece getting away from it all. On the other hand, he was responsible for the man's injury. Despite his initial reaction, Tom firmly believed that the giant had actually saved him. He had indeed reached out just as Tom had imagined, but to grab, not to push him.

His reverie ended when Katriana entered the room with yet another hot drink. Trapped by the storm and fighting the constant dampness, hot liquid punctuated the hours like those of suckling infants to the comfort of their mother's milk.

'How are you?' she asked, passing him the mug. She flopped into the big armchair and Tom swung his feet around and sat, yoga style, with the blanket still covering him and facing her.

'I feel... Fine,' he said. 'Your uncle?'

Her expression darkened. 'I don't know. He says he's OK, but that means nothing.'

'He needs to see a doctor.'

'And so do you,' she replied.

'You mentioned something about a village.'

'Lochranza. About six miles by boat or five over the mountain. Not far perhaps, but in this storm, too dangerous.'

'How long will it last?'

'As they say, you don't come here for the weather.'

Tom scanned the room for a TV. Katriana saw this and answered the question before he asked it.

'I don't know if we can get a signal, but it doesn't matter because we've no radio or TV. No forecast.'

Tom looked at the remains of the fire. 'I should relight that.'

Katriana shook her head. 'We don't have enough wood. We'll keep the one going next door for as long as we can. If it gets too cold, we can sleep on the floor in there tonight.'

Tom looked at the pathetic jumble of sticks next to the hearth. Small twigs, broken branches, the odd plank of wood splintered into manageable chunks. One thin piece had the words *Fraserborough Fish* stencilled on it in faded blue lettering.

'I could get some more. I take it that's driftwood.'

She nodded. 'Mostly. The storm will have thrown up a good supply but we should wait until it dies down. Anyway, unless we get lucky, the wood'll be wet for days.'

Over the next hour, Tom learned that Katriana was originally from Dumfries in the South but had lived in Glasgow for years. Her uncle - for that was what she continued to call him despite stumbling on the word every time she used it - still lived in their home town.

Tom tried to learn what he could about the history of their shelter, but apart from the fact that it was called Creggan Cottage, was on Arran and that a friend of her uncle owned it, Katriana was as clueless as he was.

'Why is it so important?' she asked once she realised that his persistence was driven by more than curiosity.

'It's difficult to explain,' he began. He stopped, wondering how to prevent himself sounding madder than he felt, but when he realised that that was impossible, he just came out with it. 'I've been here before.'

Katriana's eyes widened in shock. Her reaction was not what he had expected. She suddenly seemed frightened of something. And then, as quickly as the expression came, she relaxed and smiled. 'That's great, Tom. Perhaps you're local. Lochranza maybe.'

Tom shook his head. 'I mean here. Creggan Cottage. The ghosts. I can't explain how I know, but they're real.'

'What if - '

But Tom interrupted her, certain now what he wanted her to do, determined not to pause in case he lost the courage to ask her.

'Will you do something for me?' he asked.

'Of course. What?'

'This woman. She was terrified of something. Warned me to leave.' He tried to recall her words, but found himself dwelling on the image of the heart-shaped stone instead. Katriana saw him rub the tips of his fingers together as he imagined the glass-like surface slide over his skin, its cool beauty reflecting the perfect neck his mind placed it upon.

'I need to find out who she is. I... want to speak to her.'

The shocked look returned and the girl shook her head as though denying him his own thoughts.

'I want you to perform a séance,' he said. 'Now.'

ELEVEN

Katriana's refusal was emphatic. 'You don't know what you're asking, Tom.'

'I'm asking for my sanity. For your help.'

'The best help I can give is to say no.'

And so no it was.

By late afternoon the storm had abated and small patches of blue sped across the sky to the hills in the north.

The man, Calum was his name, lay awake and in pain for hours. Tom overheard a heated exchange between him and Katriana, his own name fired like bullets in the fight. When she returned from the latest bout she donned her coat, the yellow-red garment he had worn in the boat, and tossed Tom the man's. 'Let's get some wood,' she said.

Tom pitched the tarpaulin-sized jacket around his shoulders and wormed his hands through the wind-sock sleeves. The baggy tent hung below his knees and disappeared his fingers so that he had to turn the cuffs again and again to be able to see his hands.

Outside, the wind scudded above the hills, leaving the land at sea-level virtually untouched. The lazy sea undulated, spot-lit by a travelling shaft of sunlight slanting on a glittering swell of fragmented fire.

Turning right, the pair picked along the edge of the bay - a natural catchment, it seemed, for the detritus ejected by the storm - passing an enormous twisted branch, a sculptured effigy of a petrified sea monster that was too big to carry. They continued their search, clambering over weed-covered rocks that slithered and popped underfoot until they reached a tiny churning inlet, its cargo of flotsam smashed to thoughtful sizes just big enough and small enough to be perfect. Tom worked silently. Buoyed by the heady buzz of physical exercise, he and Katriana ferried their loads back to the cottage, spreading them on the 'lawn' in tidy lines to dry. Tom carried a small bundle into Calum's room and piled it in front of the fire to catch its heat.

The man glowered at him as he worked. Tom noticed this and tried to shake the belligerent stare. 'How are you feeling Mr.. eh Calum?'

The troubled face twisted in pain, his words poison darts spitting across the room. 'I'll be fine.'

Tom wanted to apologise for the incident in the dingy, but the giant turned his gaze to the ceiling and whispered, 'Close the door behind you.' Tom flickered a weak smile and left to join Katriana outside.

Spotting her lying on a column of rock, he climbed the 10 metre face to join her. The clouds continued to disperse, the occasional blue hole now a patchwork of drifting fluff and clear sky. The sun baked the flat rock, steaming its wet surface to a wispy haze, placing Katriana on a surreal bed of living stone.

'Your uncle doesn't like me.'

'He thinks you're trouble.'

'He may be right.'

The gulls were out again, this time joined by sleek white birds that Tom knew instinctively to be terns. They flew over the water, scanning the ever-quietening surface, diving suddenly on folded wings and dagger beaks to spear the sea.

The storm over, Tom looked across the water to distant hills and, shrunken by that distance, a parade of wind-generators shining like miniature, baton-twirling, majorettes.

He sat beside the girl, trying not to stare as he took in the gloss-black of her hair pillowing her head, her dark eyes squinting at the sky.

He lay back with his elbows propping him at a tilt and watched the birds. There was so much he wanted to say. The weather clearing, he was no longer trapped. He refreshed his determination to go for help. According to Katriana, there was a path over the hill. He could be in Lochranza in a few hours, looking for a boat to ferry the injured man to hospital, but when he suggested this to the girl, her answer only deepened the mystery of who she really was.

'We can look after ourselves, Tom.'

A dark cloud stood out from its white cotton-wool surroundings. Staring at it absently, the boy noted, with vague disinterest, that its individuality did not stop at its brown colour. If it wasn't for Katriana by his side, he would have been intrigued by its movement beyond the subconscious stirrings of curiosity flittering through his mind. The cloud moved towards them as its companions drifted left to the Northern Highlands. The observation bubbled close to the surface when the mass suddenly swooped right and he realised that the cloud was not a cloud, but a swarm, or a flock, or even an isolated flurry of living rain. The movement caught his attention, but his focus remained on Katriana's words.

Her independence did not surprise him. In the short time he'd known her, he expected little else.

He stared at the shifting cloud, his brain and vision momentarily coalescing to form surprise, the notion that something required his attention. As a part of him struggled with the enigma of the girl by his side and the curious event in the sky, both were interrupted by the sharp bark of a dog on the hill behind them.

Tom felt Katriana stiffen. He turned to look for the source but the girl was quicker, reacting, it seemed, with the reflexive speed of a child scalded by fire. She jumped from the rock, sinking into the pebbled beach with a gravelly crunch and ran for the cottage. She stopped and Tom saw her dilemma as she turned back towards him. They could not see the dog, but a man, rucksack on his back and a stick angled on his shoulder, descended the hill directly behind Creggan. The walker concentrated on the surety of his feet and appeared unaware of their presence.

'Quick,' said the girl under her breath. 'He can't see us.'

This statement encapsulated everything that made no sense about the girl and the companion she called her uncle. Here they were, trapped, in need of help - Tom with his aberrations and the man with his injured leg - and all Katriana could think of when help arrived was to hide.

Tom noted the panic in her eyes as she flicked her attention to the man and back to Tom. The stranger disappeared below the roof as he dropped down the steep path behind the cottage. They had seconds to act before he would emerge from the side of the building. Tom joined the girl in one easy bound, bending his knees and touching the beach with his left hand to soften the noise of the jump. Katriana grasped his hand and together they bolted for the door. Tom had no idea why they were doing this but the electric shock of Katriana's hand in his gave him something else to think of.

'Damn!' Katriana spat under her breath. Crossing the lawn, she saw the parade of drying driftwood, an advertisement for the presence she sought to conceal. She skipped over a line of wood but as she stretched for the doorknob, a cute brown and white beagle frolicked around the corner and yapped so loud and unexpectedly that Katriana cried out in fright. The dog spun on the spot and vanished the way it came. Katriana regained her momentum and threw open the door, but it was too late. A man's voice, bright as the post-storm-day, dashed the girl's hope of remaining incognito as surely as her own startled cry.

'Don't be frightened, lass. She's a bairn. She'll no touch ye.'

And, at these words, the couple stopped and turned to face the man.

TWELVE

Katriana's grip on Tom's hand tightened. She whispered through clenched teeth as they turned. 'Stay quiet.'

She continued to hold his hand even as the dog returned to spin in circles at her feet. The girl took a deep breath, straightened and smiled at the man. 'Ooh, she's adorable,' She stooped to pick up a piece of drying driftwood that had once been part of a deckchair in Ireland and tumbled it in a lazy arc through the air. In doing so, she dropped Tom's hand, his palm suddenly cold and empty.

The dog leapt, missed the catch, spun and arched its back like a swimming otter and, in one continuously fluid motion, disappeared in a brown and white blur of energy after the stick.

'That's it,' the man said. 'Ye'll no get rid of her now.'

'She's gorgeous,' said Katriana, her smile vaporising the dregs of the stubborn storm.

Closer to them now, Tom saw that the thing angled over the visitor's shoulder was actually a pick-axe. The man, red-bearded and ruddy-faced, shucked his sack from his shoulders and dropped it to the ground. The dog streaked in, dumped its trophy at the girl's feet, sat down and wiped the grass with its tail. 'What's her name?' Katriana asked as she retrieved the chair leg. Tom folded his arms.

'Sparky. A right wee bundle of fire, she is.' At the mention of her name, Sparky's eyes swivelled to her master and back to the girl, the tempo of her metronomic tail rising from a slow waltz to the frenzied thump, thump, thump of a Muppet's drumbeat.

Katriana arced the chair leg into the sea with Aboriginal skill.

The man nodded his red beard to the cottage. 'You folks staying here?'

The girl glanced at Tom and lied with a consummate ease he had not seen before. 'My mother's thinking of buying the cottage. We're on a sort of test drive.'

In the same breath she quickly added 'Digging for gold?' and Tom could not help seeing the question as a ploy to control the conversation - to park it in a safe zone. He shifted his weight from his left leg to his right, uncrossed and crossed his arms again.

The man chuckled and Tom bit his lower lip. First, Katriana had tried to convince him that the cottage belonged to a friend of her uncle and now she and her mother were on a mission to buy it. Until now, he had suspected her of lying but now he knew it.

Help stood in front of them and Katriana threw a stick and laughed and lied like a con-woman. He was struck by the contrast between her inept, little-girl performance earlier and the smiling trickster he saw now.

'If there's gold out here, I'd know about it,' the beard chuckled. 'Naw, hen. Just checking the storm's left us wi' a path.'

Tom sensed a movement by the window. The man did too and almost saw Calum's twisted face as he ducked in pain to the side of the glass.

'Just coming, mum!' Katriana shouted and then threw the stick again and said. 'I hope the path's OK.'

'I never knew Ferguson was selling,' the stranger said, rolling a cigarette.

Katriana put a hand to her mouth. 'Oh, God,' she cried. 'Don't say anything. I don't think I was supposed to tell.'

'Relax lass. Me 'n' the old codger don't exactly meet at the same parties. Anyhow, I'd rather see you folks on my way past here than him any day.'

With another tossed stick, the man hoisted his pack, angled his pick-axe again and left, Sparky skittering back and forward along the path, unwilling to leave her new best friend but worried by the fading smell of doggy treats. At last she followed her belly, carrying it and her excited yap in fading staccato bursts away from Creggan. Katriana waved and Tom stood with a pasted and uncomfortable smile on his face. The silence of their passing was filled by the gurgle of a nearby stream running happily to the sea, the gentle lap of the outgoing tide and the squeaking door as Katriana opened it to check on Calum.

Tom grasped her wrist. 'What are you doing?'

Instead of answering him, she spun on her heels. 'Wait here,' she commanded and ran inside. Incredulous, Tom stared after her and then at the retreating worker as he dwindled slowly along the storm-tattered path.

Resisting the urge to follow her, Tom found a spot by the stream and waited out his anger. This anger was directed as much at himself as the girl. He felt a fool standing like a dumb attendant during the girl's performance and the feeling chewed at his guts trying to get out. In the distance the tiny figure stopped and as Tom watched, swung his pick-axe like an animated icon for men at work.

When Katriana joined him, Tom was ready to burst.

Sitting on a rock, he stoned the stream with venomous thrusts, killing his anger as though it lived among the pebble-strewn bed.

She sat beside him and Tom let fly.

'Is anything you say the truth?'

'You don't understand.'

'No, *you* don't understand. If that man has a mobile, we could have help here just like that?' He snapped the fingers of his left hand and looked at her coldly. 'You'd better give me a good reason not to catch up with him.'

Katriana's horrified gaze looked at the distant figure and back to Tom.

'You can't tell anyone about us.'

'Ever? Is that it? Even when I get out, I just forget that I ever saw you? How can I get help without saying anything?

'What's wrong, Katriana?' And then with a flash of satisfaction, Tom saw Katriana's composure crinkle as he said,

'He's not your uncle, is he?'

Katriana looked away again and stayed silent.

'You can't even say the word without tripping on it, Katriana. This isn't your cottage or even a friend's. Calum doesn't want me here because I might spoil whatever's going on.'

That did it.

'Whatever's going on? What's that supposed to mean?'

Tom swung round to face her head-on. 'I'm not your enemy, but how can I avoid talking about you? It's ridiculous. He needs help even if he's too stubborn to accept it. If his leg's not set properly, he could be crippled for life.'

Katriana's belligerent tone softened to a quiet whisper. 'He won't listen.'

'What if I just do it? Whatever happens I'll be out of here soon.

If I can't phone, then it's over the hill. You said the path led to the village. I could be there tonight. We could have a doctor or maybe the police with a boat – '

'No. No police!'

The girl's voice reflected the panic in her eyes. Tom reeled back with the ferociousness of her outburst.

'What's going on, Katriana? What is he? A criminal?'

Katriana's mouth twisted into a grimace that broke through the mask she'd worn since the boy had met her. It was moulded by bitter experience, an automated response to his accusation.

'A criminal,' she spat. 'Yes. That's exactly what they're saying, but I've got another name for it.'

Tom took her hands in his and looked into her dark eyes. They sparkled as they filled with liquid misery. He resisted the urge to comfort her, reluctant to stop the flow. He squeezed her fingers gently and urged her to go on.

'According to half the country, he's a criminal, but I just call him father.'

THIRTEEN

Katriana shed her lies like scales of armour.

She was raised close to the small town of Plockton on the North West coast of Scotland. Not Dumfries. She was an only child, her parents, as far as she knew, happy. Katriana attended a small school where everyone knew everyone else. She lived on the far side of Loch Glenshaw where her father operated a modest salmon farm. They were not wealthy - her father refused to use the hormones that made his competitor's fish grow at five times their normal rate. Eventually he had found a niche in the health-conscious public who could afford the higher prices he was forced to charge.

Tom somehow knew this. As Katriana talked over the sound of the happy stream, the words she used took shape and colour in his mind. Red for a lie and green for truth. Even as he looked into her eyes, a hazy, half-thought saw the words *Beauty* and *Danger*, flit through the air between them like wind-blown leaves of emerald.

And so Tom learned that Calum had struggled for ten years to make his business work until finally they were settled, their struggles behind them. Katriana's father took her across the loch each morning to meet the school bus and collected her in the evening. She would often help with some of the chores like pouring feed or cleaning equipment. At weekends she would have her friends to stay or overnight with them in Plockton.

They were happy. Everyone was happy. Or so Katriana thought. Her mother, Sophia, kept her dissatisfaction quiet until one sunny day she announced that she had met someone else and was leaving home.

The change in her father was dramatic. A giant of a man, the girl had only seen his strength, but as the courts first took his home and then his farm and finally his daughter from him, he crumbled to a dishevelled wreck she barely recognised.

Green leaves swirled in non-existent gusts around the girl but she did not seem to notice them and to Tom they were no more than passing trees on a journey through a forest - in front of his eyes but buried in his mind. He flicked at them with an automatic hand as though buzzed by a half-noticed fly.

Katriana had moved to Edinburgh with her mother to live with her new boyfriend. The man's name was Viktor, a Croatian-born businessman. How he met his mother when they occupied such different worlds, Katriana did not know. He was charming and good to Katriana, but the girl could not settle in Edinburgh. She missed her friends, she missed her freedom, but most of all, she missed her father.

Forced to sell the farm, Calum moved to the city to be near his daughter, but things were never the same. He would take her to the park or walk around the castle; but gone was the gruff fun-loving man filled with purpose and life, stolen by a shell that laughed only to sound normal in front of his daughter.

A year after the split, Katriana's mother took her on holiday to Viktor's home town of Zagreb. It was beautiful, but Katriana was unaware of the real purpose behind the visit. She met his family and, despite the upset, loved the country and its people.

It was two months after they got back, as spring flowers bloomed in Princes Street Gardens, that her mother told her they were moving to Croatia.

'I cried forever. My father shouted at my mother, at Viktor, and finally, two days before we were due to leave, we ran away. Dad tried to get the court to stop the move, but mum had custody. She could live wherever she liked.'

According to Katriana, Sophia had told her daughter that she would still see her father during the holidays. He would still be a part of her life. But Katriana recalled the same words when they had moved to Edinburgh. It was a lie and their daughter knew it.

At first they slept in the car, burying themselves in quiet country roads, often in forests, sometimes by a loch. They ate chocolate and drank pop. Eventually they dumped the car when the media took up the story. A nationwide hunt tracked what they called a dangerous and unstable absent father. According to the headlines, he had kidnapped the carefree youngster. The distraught mother was leaving the country to escape his irrational behaviour. She was frightened for her own safety, they had said, but more so, for that of her daughter.

The pair took a train to Ardrossan and crossed on a crowded ferry full of tourists to the Island of Arran. Her father remembered the seldom-used cottage from their island treks. They walked in overnight, found Creggan empty and broke a window latch in the back. That was two weeks ago. They felt safe. Her father borrowed the boat which had been turned upside down on the ramp. He found the engine in the outhouse and left Katriana as he gathered supplies from Lochranza.

'We knew it couldn't last forever,' she said and her words faded to wisps of air. 'But when you arrived, it upset everything.'

Tom didn't know what to say. Perhaps he should have felt guilty, but he didn't. He had no family that he could remember and was actually jealous of the girl with two parents arguing over who should live with her. He remembered, through the delirium of his arrival, the reaction of her father and he now understood what a shock it must have been to him. Reports of a man and a girl in a remote cottage rescuing a boy would be a catastrophe, but still they could not turn him away either.

'That's why he risked the storm,' Tom said. 'He tried to convince me he was on his own when it was obvious he wasn't.'

Tom now understood and sympathised with their plight, but he could not just leave them without asking for help at the village. A doctor would surely lead to the police and, try as he might, the boy could not figure a way around the dilemma. Unless the man's condition improved over the next few hours, he would ignore both their calls for silence. He would walk over the hill and bring help whether they wanted it or not.

Tom bit back the urge to tell her this. He looked up at the hill and picked out the path cutting up and right, across its belly like a drunken surgeon's scar. It was getting late. Starting now would be an unnecessary risk. He would give them the night and in the morning, if Calum was no better, he would walk out and bring them a doctor. And to hell with the consequences.

FOURTEEN

When Katriana had finished telling Tom the truth about her father, the pair became silent in each other's company. Neither wanted the silence, but it was there just the same, awkward - a cloud of irrational fog hanging in the air that stopped them from saying what they meant. They tried, of course. 'I'm so sorry,' said Tom, glancing briefly at the liquid satin of the stream. He touched her hands as they lay clasped on her lap and meant the words as they left his mouth. But the sentiment was confused by selfish thoughts he was too ashamed of to voice.

Talk of family, of parents fighting each other for her love, awoke in Tom a longing to belong. To be loved as the girl was.

And watching Creggan Cottage over Katriana's shoulder, listening to the gurgling water by his side, the nearby sea and the birds, that longing tried to find its home in this place, as though Katriana and he were family and he had found his way home.

He hugged her as twin tears tracked her beautiful and tragic skin and she hugged him back. Seconds later, with the smell of her hair dwarfing the coconut smell of yellow broom, she pulled away to check on her father.

Tom walked the beach. He skimmed stones and then retook his perch on the small rock-tower he and the girl had shared before Sparky had interrupted them. He turned his back on the sea and looked at Creggan, searching for the source of familiarity he felt earlier. He was as certain as ever that he had been here before and now that he knew that his hosts were squatters, he wondered about its current owner. Ferguson, pick-axe-man had said. The name meant nothing to him. Tom's was Corven - he recognised that sure enough, so he would definitely recall another if there was a strong link.

Probably.

No, the name meant nothing - but this place did.

He stared and stared at the building, trying to tease the feelings he had to the surface. Occasionally he would feel the fishing line in his brain snag a thought, but as he plucked a juicy fact from his subconscious, it would slip the hook, leaving him more certain than ever that he was right and that somehow he belonged here.

Neither Katriana nor Tom avoided each other, but by the time she finished her ministrations, the barrier was thick with that awkward and invisible fog.

Unable to sit still, Tom stood atop the rocky plinth and looked at the hill beyond the cottage. Drifting patches of shadow lazed over the bright green and brown skin of the small mountain. The path, a light-green line where it was grassy and brown where it was not, ran up from the cottage for 50 metres before turning right. To Tom, it was suddenly a lifeline that joined him to a world he never knew - the world that brought Sparky and her friendly master to them. He looked left, searching for the man-at-work but he had moved on, the coast empty and wild and... and... something. That *almost* something, teasing him like a tickle in his head he couldn't scratch.

Returning to the hill, another *something* caught his eye at the point where the path turned right. A pile of stones, too ordered to be accidental, lay to the left of the curve. Tom jumped to the ground, made his way to the side of the cottage and climbed the hill.

An old ruin, barely a small complex of rectangular waist-high walls overlooked Creggan. The stream ran underground here, a pleasing backdrop to the serene and peaceful locale. Tom picked his way through bracken and ankle-twisting clumps of heather.

As he did, and as he neared the ruin, his eyes watered as though a small gust of wind gritted his vision. He rubbed them, aware that there was no such wind, no swirling dust - no grit to make him cry.

The smell of wood-smoke drifted from Creggan and somehow gave life to the ruin so that Tom could almost imagine its ancient inhabitants huddled over a fire as another frustrated storm battered ineffectually at the walls. The same unassailable walls that lay now as straight-lined jumbles of grey stone.

Looking down on Creggan's roof, to the slightly sighing sea, to the distant hills and the never-ending sky, Tom did not find the view from the ruin beautiful; it broke his heart.

Those inexplicable tears dropped to his cheeks but Tom did not notice them. A sound, faint at first, caused him to turn on the spot. A soft sigh and then a song. A woman's voice seemed to rise from the subterranean stream and fill the air with sweet music. And then a violin, a fiddle, haunting the air like the plaintive cry of a lover lost to her love.

An overwhelming sense of sadness and joy followed Tom through the ruin and he felt then as though he never wanted to leave this place for the rest of his life.

Beyond the walls, the hill rose steeply, the building itself on a flat step that formed a natural terrace; perfect for a small croft. A cluster of rocks caught Tom's eye. About twenty metres from the top left corner, it seemed to draw from him another sensation, a sensation that turned the joy of his discovery to a dread that closed the doors on whatever feelings they stirred deep within him. He stared and the plaintive strings became a screech and then a scream that fell to Katriana's call, beckoning him back to the cottage.

FIFTEEN

With the shadow of dusk racing over him, white smoke floating in an unbending column from the chimney and the smell of bacon in the air, Tom left the strange pile of stones and joined Katriana to eat.

The smoke, it turned out, was from a mix of partially dried wood and the remnants of the pre-storm supply.

A small driftwood tepee hissed and popped in the hearth and Katriana sat in the armchair as Tom, suddenly ravenous, gulped a handful of rashers and beans as though he hadn't eaten for days.

'Sorry,' she said, nodding to his plate. 'Dad was supposed to bring supplies back in the boat.' The word *dad* seemed light on her lips.

'This is good,' Tom muttered between mouthfuls. 'Really good.' Of course he needed about ten times the amount she had served him, but he was grateful just the same.

Finished, he ran a finger around the plate and sucked the flavour from his skin. Katriana hardly touched hers. Despite himself, Tom could not resist a hungry glance at her meal as she placed it on a small coffee table and sat back in her seat.

'Take it.'

Tom felt like a beggar and hesitated. 'Please,' she continued. 'I'm not hungry.'

Seconds later, Katriana's plate was empty and at last the boy felt as though he had dulled the pangs cramping his stomach.

Desperate for something to say, he asked about her father. Listening to the fevered moan boring through the wall, Tom could guess the answer, but he asked anyway.

'I'm worried. He won't have it though, Tom. He's frightened they'll take me away.'

'It's got to happen sometime. You said yourself. The whole nation is on the lookout for you. You can't stay here forever and as soon as you're seen together, that's it.'

Katriana didn't answer. He could see the defeat on her face.

'Look, Tom. I'm sorry I lied, but you don't know what it's like to have your parents - ' She stopped then and looked suddenly guilty. 'I'm sorry. I didn't mean that.' The ice thawed, Katriana's black hair catching a line of reflected light as the fire suddenly broke through some barrier and became a healthy blaze.

'You know,' she said. 'Once you're out, you'll be home soon enough. Someone's bound to have reported you missing.'

Tom leant forward, his heart and thoughts flitting between this moment with Katriana, his determination to get help and the Creggan dreams that seemed to beckon him like beautiful and hellish sirens.

'I don't need to leave here to find out.'

The look he gave her was enough. She understood immediately what he was saying without him needing to ask.

'You know, my aunt could have been wrong.'

'Then she's wrong. Will you do it?'

Katriana looked around the room and shivered. 'This place,' she said. 'You can almost taste the past.' She paused then and the house seemed to sigh as a downdraft fell on the fire and the roof groaned at the night air cooling its wooden bones. This time, however, if she was frightened, the fear did not stop her.

'I've always wondered,' she began. 'I suppose I'll never have a better reason to try.'

She looked at Tom, her held breath a brief pause in time. Tom remained still and silent. And the tepee fire crackled to life.

'OK,' she said at last. 'We'll do it.' She stood and grasped the two plates from the table, but before she could make whatever preparations she thought necessary, Tom spoke softly as though he didn't want to break Katriana's cooperative mood.

'Not here,' he said. 'The ruin above the cottage.'

Katriana thought about this, standing with the plates in her hands and backlit by the fire.

'Why?'

'I... don't know for sure. I just sort of know without knowing anything. It's a feeling that's all.' As he spoke, he heard the music in his head, the fiddle, the haunting cry.

Katriana nodded. 'Fine,' she agreed. 'The ruin it is.'

After checking on Calum, they wrapped themselves warm, Tom in a dark fleece belonging to Katriana, Katriana in the pink jumper she had worn on the edge of the boiling sea. It was surprisingly warm outside, a full moon and sparse fluffy clouds giving the land a definition beyond the gloom he had seen before.

Somewhere above them a deer barked. Tom took a gas lantern, its hiss a constant and unchanging note that drowned the sounds of the stream, his thumping heart and Katriana's rhythmic breath as they climbed the hill.

The light from the lamp formed a bubble around them. It was so bright that when holding it, arm stretched in front, Tom was partially blinded by its intensity. He brought it down to his side where it threw his own shadow to the left and Katriana's to the right.

Soon they reached the ruin, the clumpy heather threatening to trip them with every step. The hiss of the lamp seemed to fade over time despite its constancy.

Perhaps it was anticipation, nerves or excitement, but on entering the cloistered walls of the ruin, Tom felt the same mixture of dread and joy he had felt earlier. The answer to who he was lay right here - in this place. And tonight he would learn exactly what that answer was.

SIXTEEN

Tom wasn't sure what to expect, but the word *séance* formed a vague impression of a circle of hands. He was not surprised then, when Katriana reached across and, as they faced each other, grasped his in hers and told him to close his eyes.

They had picked a spot near the centre that could have been a living or cooking area. There was a hole in the wall facing the hill - the remains of a fireplace or a smoke vent.

Inside the structure, the grass was soft, trimmed by sheep whose droppings had to be kicked out of the way before they sat down. The wall facing the sea was almost gone so that, if Tom looked slightly to his left and Katriana to her right, they could see small clumps of twinkling light on the far Ayrshire shore.

Katriana's hands felt cool in his. They interlocked fingers and the girl spoke in a hushed voice. 'Whatever you do, don't break the link.'

She whispered something under her breath. Tom tried to hear it, but soon drifted into his own thoughts when he realised that he couldn't make out anything she said. Her whispers mingled with the hiss of the lamp and the nearby subsurface gurgle. He imagined the music he had heard earlier in his head and it appeared to materialise around him as he did. So too the singing. A single voice, quietly, as if to a child.

Once there was a Bonnie wee Bairn,
He sat upon my knee,
Says I to him, my own wee kin,
I'll tell ye all ye need to ken,
There's ne'er a mithir, or love fer another,
Than the love of yer mither, that's me …

Unknown to Tom, he swayed with the rhythm of the song. It played again and again, drawing him ever deeper into another world. In this world he was a young boy, his mother at once rocking him to sleep and then singing as he bounced on her lap. And soon he saw a younger self, in his imagination, sitting by the fire, a girl, his own youthful age, bright red hair and gleaming dark eyes, tapping her feet as she bowed a fiddle, the tune and the hiss and the song and the whispers coalescing to a frenzied whirl of sound.

It surrounded Tom, engulfed him in its closeness, its hypnotic grip, its visceral energy.

So lost was he to the sound that it became more than imagination. He was there - in that room - not just watching the family gathering, but part of it. The fire crackled loudly, its light softening the rough texture of stone walls. Shadowed wooden beams propped the roof and a musty smell of dampness and baking was curiously pleasant in the sing-song air.

He opened his eyes, certain that he would be in that room still, disappointed to find that he was not. Katriana's hands continued to grip his, her quiet voice muttering, head bent and oblivious to Tom's vision. He returned to its embrace and quickly retook his place in the happy dream.

Tess bowed her fiddle and her mother and Tom sung. Tom had no idea how he knew the girl's name was Tess, but he did and accepted her label without question. Outside, beyond the resurrected walls, another storm blasted the building as fierce as the one that had trapped them so recently. This memory - his time with Katriana, her hands holding his now, the family scene - all images bubbling inside him, bringing with them wave after wave of sweet intense emotion. Tom could have died happy there and then.

Later, perhaps, he would wish he had.

As Tom embraced the comfort and security, the warmth of the fire, the pleasant fury of the storm at bay, another sensation drew him from the logic that so recently constrained him. The feeling began with that same notion of familiarity – he had seen the woman before, knew the girl's name, Creggan Cottage, the ruin - but as the intoxicating sound ensnared his heart as tightly as his thoughts, the root of this familiarity shifted. He *knew* her - Yes. But the word *knew* was inadequate, weak. Rather, Tom wallowed in a sensation that engulfed him with its intensity; an intensity that changed his life. He searched for the word to match the emotional assault on his new-born world but, to do so, a part of him had to leave its cover to enter the dry realm of words. The candidates - linguistic objects - swum around his head: *Familiarity, Fear, Anger, Anguish* - a procession of words lining up for consideration, his mind resisting the intrusion. *Loneliness, Friendship, Family...*

And then he had it; the one word that pushed through them all - the word that could change everything - Love.

SEVENTEEN

Love. All powerful. Consuming. Dangerous.

Katriana's hands closed tighter on Tom's, suddenly hot, suddenly part of the phantom fabric engulfing them. He looked up from his place by the fire and there she was, standing before him, holding his hands. She let go and drifted round to look at Tess, at the woman singing her lullabies. There was no feeling of loss when Katriana broke away, they somehow seemed connected still so that Tom knew they remained together in the séance beyond the wonderful illusion he hoped would never end.

Katriana's shadow danced with the firelight as though taken by the music. She looked back at Tom and smiled. 'This is Love,' she said. 'I feel it.' Her long black hair swayed with her head as she listened to the woman's voice. She took Tom's hands again and together they spun the room around them, the fiddle and the girl, the fire, the shadowed beams, the blonde-haired woman.

And then he was with that woman. *That woman* - his mother. The impossibility of this fact ignored. Coddled in her arms, he seemed tiny then, his protector grown to an Amazonian giant.

The world continued to burl. Tom nuzzled her chest, giggling as he tried to stop his head flying outwards with the happy force of it all. And in front of him, the heart-shaped pendant. His left hand went to it and felt its cool smoothness in his fingers, saw himself in another time rubbing it and rubbing it, threading it with string, placing it around a white and pure neck, the neck his small arms now embraced in this dizzy, giddy world.

They danced and sang for what seemed like hours and then the room melted away and a slightly older Tom lay warm in bed, the woman, blonde hair tickling his cheeks as she bent to kiss him, her pendant swaying back and forward like a hypnotist's charm drawing him to sleep, his eyes closing beyond closed eyes.

The small boy dreamt then and Tom shared the dream with him. He was running along the beach he recognised as the semi-bay outside Creggan. The sun shone, a stiff but pleasant breeze pushing his long brown hair back like a horse's mane, rising and falling as he vaulted stone and driftwood.

He turned his head, laughing aloud. Tess grabbed his arm and spun him to face her. Her frame was slight, but she could run, her grip like jaws. Still, he shook himself free and ran on, turning to his right to see Katriana at his side and laughing with equal abandon. And even then, as his arms pistoned at his sides, he felt the warmth of Katriana's hands in his, back at the séance, sitting in the night, the lamp casting their shadows over the ruin, an invisible bond tying one to the other as they ran.

Dodging another lunge from Tess, he swung back towards Creggan, but noted, with mild curiosity, that the white cottage was not there. He looked up the hill to the left and saw the edge of the ruin. Although, it wasn't a ruin. It was home. Tom's mind did not lurch at this thought. It was home. Of course it was. So what?

In the clearing that should have housed Creggan Cottage, the blonde woman he knew as *Mother* sat scribbling thoughtfully onto what looked like hard yellow paper. She dipped a small stick with a metalled top into a pot and scribbled some more. Hearing the children's laughter, she looked up and squinted against the sun. 'Careful, Tess. You'll hurt him.'

Hurt him? Ridiculous. At that moment, Tom was invincible and no-one, least of all a slip of a girl he could outrun and out-jump, could hurt him.

But as he tumbled to the ground in happy breathlessness, something inside Tom knew that this thought was not right. A slow dread rose from his stomach and he denied it like suppressed vomit at a joyous party.

He looked at his mother, determined that his time with her should not be spoiled. Not this time. Not again.

His mother stiffened and stared in dismay beyond the rock pillar out to sea.

A small white sail cracked like a gunshot as a boat swung around in the suddenly ugly wind. Tom knew why his mother's heart fell, but could not bring himself to dredge the thoughts from that part of him that knew and bring them to this divine and sacred place. Nevertheless, the boat sailed closer and the woman jumped to her feet. 'Inside,' she ordered.

Tom and Tess stood their ground. The young girl stared at the boat, her hands on her hips. Defiant.

'Tessa. Tom. Please.' The woman took their arms and gently pushed them towards the small path leading up to the grey stone cottage and the pair reluctantly moved.

'Stay where you are,' a booming voice called from the sea. 'What are you doing, woman? I've equipment and supplies to shift.'

Tom watched the boat run fast to the shore. As it did, the sail dropped and the small vessel's momentum carried it up the beach with the grinding crunch of keel parting stone.

Tess started back down the hill, her mother looking fearfully from her children to the boat.

Tom stood still, watching the man as he half-vaulted, half-fell to the pebbled land. He was not surprised now to sense the familiarity with which he greeted the stranger despite that part of him that tried to kill the recognition before it found its rightful place in his memory.

'Don't stand there. Give me a hand.'

Automated, Tom followed Tess and they both hauled the boat up the beach, Tess' strength matching his, the boat surprisingly light despite the pile of boxes stowed throughout its bulk.

Tom tried to see the man's face, but his back was to him. He moved strangely and at first Tom thought it was the water at his shins that made him shuffle in awkward stumbling bursts, but even before he turned, before he crunched up the beach and tossed the trio a scowl, the boy knew that that wasn't true in just the same way he seemed to know everything else.

The man was thin, half bent and with a gait that had one leg dragging the other. His face - mouth covered by a scarf despite the sun - was the face of a man in pain. His eyes screwed up, his flesh twitching sporadically as though tiny needles crawled beneath its surface. His skin, mottled red with white patches, hung leprous in small clumps from his cheeks and forehead. Tom felt curiously sorry for the man, but this quickly turned to dread again as he swivelled his eyes on him and said, 'Boy. You lied to me. Why did you lie to me?'

And even though the man did not move from the spot, Tom felt the lash of a whip on his back, the tear of muscle as a non-existent barb drew across his shoulders, the ooze of blood soaking his shirt. He fell to his knees and his mother and the girl ran to comfort him and they fell too and Katriana looked at the man with hatred in her beautiful dark eyes.

EIGHTEEN

Still on that phantom coast, Katriana ran to Tom's side and tried to haul him to his feet. She grasped his hands and pulled on him. Her fingers wrapped his and then let go. Still they remained connected, even though the boy was now on his own, floating skywards, looking down on the beach and then on the ruin that was yet again a ruin. There, a boy and a girl – Tom and Katriana - sat facing each other. They were struggling, the girl trying to wrench herself from the boy's grasp, her hair flailing her head and shoulders like black satin strips. It was dark, the only light, that from a hissing sun by the couple's side.

Tom floated down to take a closer look and, as he did, he heard music, felt the soft embrace of his mother's arms, saw the gentle sway of a stone heart lull him awake. He opened his little-boy eyes and felt the comfort of his bed, then opened them again and saw Katriana's fear as she jumped to her feet and looked around her, her hands at last free, her feet backing away from something she couldn't see.

Tom stepped towards her and took her shoulders. 'He's gone. Katriana. He's gone.'

She stared, wide-eyed, at him and then at his hands. Tom was a silhouette against the lamp at his back, his outline a bright series of ruffled curves, his face a featureless black shadow.

Katriana continued to back away.

'Did you see them?' Tom asked. Katriana nodded her head.

'Who are they?' She looked around the ruin, their isolation suddenly absolute beyond the false security of the gaslight.

They were at the wall overlooking Creggan's roof, Katriana backed as far as she could go and Tom's hands now gentle on her arms. She was shaking and Tom drew himself closer to hug the fear from her body. But holding her in his arms did more than that. The wool under his fingers was at once textured and soft, the hair at his cheek, cool and fragrant, her breath on his neck, hot.

Katriana lifted her head and looked at Tom, her shaking body calmed to the rhythm of slow and deep breathing. Beyond the girl's eyes - a gaze that should have been impossible to break - the light surrounding them flickered curiously and Tom stiffened. Dawn suddenly washed the coast - a dawn with no rising sun on the horizon. He squinted at the sky directly overhead and there it was, faint at first, but soon glowing bright, drowning the lamp and warming his face with a beautiful and unscheduled day.

Below them, Creggan Cottage dimmed to a haze and then to nothing. The small sail-boat was there again, keeled over to its side, its cargo gone. Behind Tom, further up the hill, a man screamed in anger.

'You'll do as I say.'

Tom whipped around, releasing his grip on Katriana. The stone cottage was rebuilt but somehow he could see beyond, as though it was constructed of glass, to the small clump of rocks on the other side.

Somewhere in another world, Katriana called to him but she was too faint to register. The boy crossed the ruin, walking through vapour walls as he did.

Standing at the rocks, the man dragged Tom's mother to a black patch that could have been a hole formed by adjacent boulders not quite touching. Tess, as if from nowhere, flew at the man and Tom's heart leapt as he saw her target fall, his grip on the woman's arm lost. Despite his awkward movements, the attacker was on his feet in a blur. An object, short and thin like an extended aerial, appeared in the man's hands. He raised it high and brought it down hard and fast on the girl's face. Before it connected, in that split second of air, an inch from her skin, an arc of electricity leapt across the gap and ran around Tess' head, crowning her in a kaleidoscope of shimmering silver barbs. She screamed and Tom lurched forward, ignoring Katriana's call from another dream.

As he reached them, Tom's mother grabbed the rod and yelled in pain as her hand twitched and sparked; the smell of roast meat sickening the air between them.

'Leave her alone,' Tom yelled. The man ignored him. Tess lay on the ground unconscious, his mother's body writhing in agony as her hand sizzled and fumed. Tom tried to run towards them, his feet useless blocks of stone. He was frightened of the man, of course, but that had nothing to do with his helplessness. At that moment, any fear he had was for his mother and for Tess. He knew with absolute certainty that if he could get close enough, he would somehow find the strength to overcome the beast and stop him hurting his family. His soul.

And then his mother's attacker leaned over her, grabbed her dress at the front, scrunching the fabric and the pendant. He pushed his face to hers. 'Do not question me, woman. Ever!'

He no longer wore his scarf and, closer now, Tom could see that he was brutally disfigured. The boy felt no pity, unmoved by his hideous look. More terrible still was the hatred in his eyes as he dragged the woman into the rock, her hands slipping from his wrists and falling limp by her sides.

The man shifted his grip and Tom saw the string around his mother's neck tighten like a garrotte and then pop; it and the pendant slipping to the ground, pummelled by stamping boots as first his mother and then Tess disappeared into the hole.

NINETEEN

Tom stood in the darkness for the two seconds it took him to readjust to his new reality. He was back in the ruin, Katriana shaking him in small bursts and then letting him go as though scared of catching the terror their union had brought to her mind.

'Tom! Come away from here.'

For Tom, the taste of burnt flesh lingered in his nostrils. He could not shake the sense of his mother's helplessness, the image of a white-hot crown searing Tess' head. He ran for the rocks, scrambling blindly beyond the light of the lamp, bashing a knee on a crumpled wall, falling and stumbling and running until he reached the place that seconds before had staged his worse nightmare. 'Tom, there's no-one there,' the girl yelled. But when he continued to ignore her, she grasped the lamp and picked her way up the hill to join him.

As the light caught up with him, Tom squatted on his knees. Without a word, he reached back and Katriana placed the handle in his grasp. He swung it forward and pushed the hissing cylinder inside the tiny enclave. There was no vast cavern, nowhere for the man to have disappeared to.

The feeling of certainty was so strong that Tom was bemused by the dank shallow hollow that stretched no more than the length of a grave from dark entrance to cold wall.

'I saw him. He was here!'

'Who, Tom?'

But Katriana had seen too. *The man in the boat.* She knew by the fear in the boy's eyes - the determination in his voice - that he was talking about the creature with the covered face and cruel stare.

She was tempted to tell him that it was a dream, but how could she? She had conjured the demon during the séance after all.

Tom scrabbled in the darkest corners with his fingers. He poked and scratched and tore at clumps of earth, ripping his nails and blooding his skin.

At last, when even Tom's fractured mind understood that he was getting nowhere, he sat back on his heels and Katriana saw, by the searing white of the lamp, that his face was ravaged by whatever he had witnessed in this cold, bleak spot. His cheeks were covered in dirt now too, twin lines smudging his skin on either side of his nose where flying dirt had stuck. He had the look of a ghostly girl streaked in mascara. Seeing that he was on the verge of defeat, Katriana hovered a careful hand onto Tom's arm. She touched him, lightly at first, and then took a large gulp of night air, wrapped her arms around his shoulders and drew him up to her.

Together, silent, they guided each other back to the cottage. Katriana's head spun with confusion over what had just happened. To her mind, she had unleashed a terrible nightmare on the boy. She had tried to help him but had, instead, torn him apart with a hellish vision of a past he confused with his own.

This was not how Tom saw things. Yes, he had caught a glimpse of events seared into the walls of the ruin, but it was this and more. The feelings he had were too strong to be a trick of his mind. The ruin was a conduit, the events part of who he was.

The fire was almost dead and Katriana used some of the precious dry stuff to kindle the wet. As Tom sat in a blank stare on the armchair, she left him to check on her father. When she returned, Tom was on his feet, rummaging the room with determination. He no longer looked like a wild animal cornered by death, but a hunter, in control and certain of his task.

'What are you after, Tom?'

'I don't know.' And then he looked up suddenly. 'Is there a tool shed?'

'Under the stairs,' she said. 'What...'

But Tom was already out the room and flinging open the door to the cupboard.

He then squeezed past Katriana and took the lamp from the room they had just left and thrust it into the darkness. A treasure chest of tools and brooms jumped at him and he grinned to himself.

'I know you think I'm crazy,' he said as he rummaged its contents 'but I'm not.' He pulled out a long-handled spade, turned and stared at her with calm determination. 'You saw it, Katriana. I know you did.'

'I *imagined* something,' she said, obviously unconvinced by her own words.

Tom looked at the lamp in his hands. 'Do you have a torch?' he asked. She disappeared then as he continued his search for equipment and inspiration. He settled on the spade, a small garden fork and a long knife, well beyond its useful life of hacking through jungles or Scottish bracken.

Katriana returned with an elastic-banded head-torch.

'Thanks,' he said.

'I don't know how long the battery will last.'

Tom twisted it on and a satisfying beam spread a cone of light onto the floor.

As Tom hoisted the spade over his shoulder, the light on his head and the blade and fork in his right hand, Katriana suddenly appeared conflicted. She looked to the outside door and then back to her father's. As if he had been waiting for this cue, the man moaned gently and Katriana took an automatic step to his room, cracked the door and peeked in. 'I should really..'

But Tom was already moving. 'He needs you, Katriana. Stay with him.' And then he left.

TWENTY

Everything looked different through the narrow and dim cone of the torch. Tom found the path and then focused on his feet as he climbed the hill. The still night air smelled of a childhood he couldn't quite recall. In the absence of light, the night was alive with an aromatic mix that dug deep into the past and somehow conjured a sense of mountain and moon and stars. It smelled too of the earth under his feet, the water running underground - tangible and intangible sensations evoking long lost thoughts and memories beyond his reach. Even so, as he stepped over the juddering spot-lit walls of the ruin and made his way up to the rocks, there were certain things he knew to be true.

True and impossible.

The rocks making up the pile of rubble that he thought of as home were covered in moss. How long ago they had fallen he had no idea, but the time was measured in decades, perhaps centuries.

Once again his thoughts and emotions struggled with common sense.

Nevertheless, he recalled the first time he'd seen the woman he now felt was his mother. Then, she had seemed to walk through a door - a door that splintered and reconstructed between blinks. If Tom had been hallucinating then, perhaps he'd done so again. The disfigured madman had dragged his mother and Tess through solid rock. Well, that's what happens in hallucinations, the sensible him told his other self. But Tom did not break step. He reached the spot, dropped the small tools and, still standing, probed the ground with the thin and rusted end of the spade. The noise clanged through the night and close-by a ground-nesting bird shrieked and flapped inefficient wings into the air.

He dropped to his knees, the torch beam following his eyes to light a small patch of stone and moss and animal parts. He took his blade and scraped away the moss, picked up a small dismembered leg-bone and cleared the bed in a succession of scratching dog-like throws behind him; blade in one hand, followed by the bare fingers of the other.

And then he found it. His hand, bleeding, black and patchwork-stained mossy green, flickered in and out of the bobbing, frantic light. So intent on the hellish gardening, so focused on the images that came and went in his head, that he almost missed it.

All three had stood where he knelt now. His mother, Tess - Him. Tom's heart spurred him on - a walloping sound driving his pace faster and faster still.

He recalled the scene.

Tess had knocked the man off balance and soon she herself lay twitching on the ground, the woman jumping to her aid, lightning-bright cracks turning the black shreds of shadow to fire. And she fell too, the cruel rod in her grasp, ozone and burnt beef scenting the air.

Gnarled, flaking fingers scrunched fabric in Tom's mind, the woman's head lolled back, her long blonde hair sweeping the ground, her pale neck stretched taut, throat exposed. And then the sound of tearing cloth, the pop of buttons, the guttural grunt and fury of mismanaged anger.

And he saw it then. He saw it then and felt it in his hand now. The string around her neck, digging into her flesh, a line gashing her skin, deep, as though destined to break through as the thin noose tightened and tightened more.

And snap!

It whipped from her neck, elastic and ecstatic, free, the white line now red, circling her neck, the string and pendant falling to earth, the woman somehow floating into the rock with Tess, as the stone heart hit the ground with the force of a fallen tombstone.

Tom brought his hand back from the verge of a backward throw. He slowed to a virtual stop, sensing the enormity of his find before he knew what it was, before he saw it. He recognised the feel of it and felt that recognition within himself, the knowing as profound as the vision that summoned him there, the vision that was, now and forever, much, much more.

The light from his torch now steady, Tom opened his hand and gawked at it, the polish dulled by time, but the stone heart still beautiful, still smooth and still capable of ripping him apart.

He brought the object closer to the light and picked at a tiny thread jutting from a hole running from one side of the pendant to the other. A piece of string or wound-cloth, all that remained of the disintegrated chain, slid easily from the cavity. He caressed its surface with one thumb and then another, wiping a thin film of greasy life from its surface.

The movement, this intimate act, brought him ever closer to the skin the stone had last touched. And at once the heart became the key to a part of him that was always there, but buried in some safe place that was about to be opened.

TWENTY ONE

Clutching the stone, Tom's arms circled the white neck of its owner, his mind back in the place of dreams and nightmares. He felt the happy laughter of spinning joy, his head thrown back with the exuberance of childhood. Back in the dream house, he felt the warmth of the fire, the heat of his mother's body, the smell of wood-smoke, heard the constant fiddle, the sing-song lullaby. Now though, as he spun and laughed, another image pushed its way through the happy scene. He lay in bed, the hypnotic heart swinging before his eyes and then rising, a kiss left on his forehead, the light now dimming - and darkness - the calm suddenly replaced by raised voices beyond the closed door. The words, angry and ugly, pounded against the panels, muffled by them.

Venomous sounds formed to wispy solids that drifted to the floor, through the white line under the door and reconstructed themselves on the inside of Tom's black room, ghost-words that matched the furious sounds of adults not yet killing each other.

Tom shook himself to rid the image from his mind, but really, this is what he'd hoped to find - the truth. Who he was. The stone heart in his hand plundered his memory with unrelenting efficiency. And, lying in bed, the words drifted towards him, shimmering a terrifying, ethereal power.

The young Tom sat up, watched and listened.

'Don't interfere, woman!'

And the words circled the boy's head, closed on his neck as though a noose set to strangle the life from him.

'They're children!'

And then the exasperated growl of a misunderstood man. 'They have to learn!'

The man's voice chilled and the words morphed and turned an icy blue so cold that Tom's breath became a pale vapour that crusted on contact with the sentence. 'And you have to learn, too.'

And then a scream, the words closer now, circling ever faster, the ozone and the burning, the freezing noose and Tom's hands tearing at it, his fingers burning on the ice, the warmth of his hands melting the letters, so that their substance wetted his skin to a slick liquid that seemed to spread over his palm and around each hand. Tom shook himself free and once again he floated into the air, the words and the night-time gone, the room replaced by unfocused walls and a dim light that surrounded them and came from nowhere and everywhere at the same time.

Below, a younger Tom and a younger Tess sat bound by leather belts encircling their waists, their chests, their ankles and their foreheads; fastened to strange high-backed chairs rising from ankle-deep pools of water. Barefooted, the pair waited their fates with grim determination not to cry. Tom drifted downwards, but instead of seeing from close-by as he had intended, he seemed to merge with the boy in the seat and then saw, heard and felt everything as the youngster did.

Sitting straight-backed, Tom was angled towards Tess. She looked fearless, her long red hair braided to a tight rope, tiny freckles peppering her nose and bare arms.

Tom instinctively tried to free himself, knew before he did that it was useless. To his right, Tess threw him a look and micro-shook her head. He was not to move. But, of course, he did.

It was then that the boy noticed the thing touching his head. A small, semicircular cradle, supported the back of his skull and neck, pressed tight by the strap girdling his forehead.

A tiny tingle tickled his skin where the cold metal touched him. He pulled away and the strap hauled him back.

Close to and in front of the children, the shuffling and hunched figure of their tormentor took his place in his own chair, apparently unconcerned by the struggles of the pair in front of him.

Tom raged, anger pumping through his veins as though replacing the blood that gave him life. He wrenched his head forward, pulled on his arms, kicked his feet. The boy's bonds tightened and a pain, molten steel, shot through the back of his neck as though the cradle had turned to fire. It raged through his body, in and up and down, through his head, his torso, flowing through his feet to the water at his toes.

'Stop fidgeting, boy,' the man said. 'You've done this before. Don't be a baby.'

But Tom continued to struggle, fire searing his neck and toes.

'Tom,' shouted Tess, her words as painful to her as Tom's movement was to him. 'Sit still. It's not so bad if you sit still.'

Distracted by her voice, Tom stopped struggling and the pain ceased. Tess too seemed to slump without moving and her face softened to a statuesque plea for her brother to make it easy on himself.

Her brother.

Soon the man sat opposite them, hunched across the short gap and unbuckled Tess' left arm and Tom's right. Tess seemed to know what was expected of her. She entwined her fingers with Tom's, their hands fusing as one, the girl's strength suddenly evident to the boy - a strength beyond that of her build, beyond the slip of a girl that sat beside him.

The comfort of Tess' touch was blackened by another. Stretching either side of them, the man grasped Tom and the girl's tethered and outer hands - closing the intimate circle.

The contact shocked Tom more than the pain. Without thinking he tried to turn to look at the corrupting link, but the strap tightened around his head and boiling oil flowed in his veins.

'Now, Tom,' the man said with a benign smile. 'If you're finished fooling around, we can begin.'

TWENTY TWO

Still in the dream, Tess' grip on Tom tightened as though she had just gone into spasm. At the back of his head, the brace warmed to a dull, steady glow that seemed to wash through him like a relaxing drug but, sensing Tess' anticipation, Tom knew that there was more to come and he would not like it one bit.

He expected pain, but when the thing happened, it was beyond anything he could have guessed beyond his crazy dreams. Somewhere in his head, a slight buzz grew and multiplied to a hideous hive swarming through his brain. He shook himself, an automatic reaction to the sense that a dozen insects had just crawled inside each of his ears. The straps held tight and the bees or wasps or bloated flies diverged to a polyphony of individual drones that roamed his brain, picking up and dropping off payloads as though workers sorting through an impossibly large store. Parts of his mind seemed to drift with the vibrating acoustic points. They travelled through his bones, down his arms, to Tess on one side and to the malignant fingers clutching him on the other. The sound and his thoughts became little packages flowing between the three bodies, shuttling bits of him and the girl and the man in a froth of miss-mashed egos. Information. Fragments of self - Tom's life – seemed to be by-products of plunder and Tom snatched at them.

And then he saw himself through the man's eyes. And Tess too. And he saw anger. A constant anger confused with a mix of awe and fear. Tom could not unpick the feelings, but they swirled with the furious buzzing and prickled the man's leprous skin every time he looked at the pair in the seats opposite him.

A ball of light, as large as a car, zoomed and left in an unknown sky. Words swished through black space and died. Two babies lay naked on purple heather - a hideous creature, barely alive, scooping the tiny bundles in his mottled arms.

And then the questions. Facts. Anatomy, metals, electricity, stock, chemistry, nanotech, tools, money. The hive swarmed and plundered and drained the boy of life until he could take no more and lapsed into unconsciousness.

Tom awoke to the sound of his mother's voice. It repeated a phrase he'd heard before.

Under the hag stone, he seemed to remember the beautiful ghost in his mind tell him. But with each repeat, it changed and cleared to become something different. Clearer and clearer still until the phrase was Chinese-whispered to something else.

Under the hat stone, the heargstone. The Hearthstone.

Under the heart stone.

The light was dim now. Kneeling on the ground above the ruin, Tom looked at the object in his hand. The heart stone. The stone he made for his mother.

Fighting the crippling image of his mother in the hands of the beast, his sister Tess in the chair and the buzzing drones in his head, he probed the ground at the point he'd found the pendant. Nothing made sense to him, but if there was the slightest chance of saving his mother he had to try. She was dead, he knew that. She was a ghost and so was his sister. But then he was alive and so they could be too. Whipping the band from his head, he pushed the torch close to the ground and saw it immediately. A tiny recess, partially hidden under a flap streaked in Tom's blood, scratched by his shredded nails. It looked like a stone but was a hinged cover, hiding a rusted handle like a horse's stirrup, upside down, its shaft buried in the ground. Shaking fingers - blood and grime-encrusted - curved under the cold metal. Tom pulled, lightly at first, but nothing happened. He tried again, this time using a strength he did not know he possessed. He positioned himself, knees either side, right hand gripping his wrist, the fingers of his left curled around the bar and he focused his universe on that one spot until the metal groaned, screaming through the darkness as though he had broken its bones. The returning silence stretched like cotton wool over the mountains, even as a hole as big as a grave sank into the ground on a sloping floor that ramped down and inside the mountain.

Tom jumped to his feet and stepped away from the opening. He took his torch and swung the beam forward, sticking his head out to peer as far as he could into the hole.

He listened and heard nothing. The night had stopped, the sounds in his head gone, the moment an infinite pause in the universe before some cosmic event Tom could not fathom.

He turned towards the cottage, hidden beyond the lip of the grass terrace. Ayrshire still twinkled at him - a merry hint of normality that belonged to everyone, it seemed, except to him.

He walked down the hill, stopped and looked back up at the rocks. He should tell Katriana in case anything happened. But what could she do? This was his problem. He'd already brought her enough trouble. If he was sensible, he could have a quick look, stay close to the surface and be back in minutes.

Knowing full well that he was kidding himself, he turned back up the hill, repositioned the torch on his head, edged towards the ramp and walked slowly into the mountain.

TWENTY THREE

The tunnel air was foetid - warmer than the cool night on the surface. Tom looked over his shoulder as he descended the ramp and took a last look at the sky; a dark slit between the roof and upward-sloping floor where his torchlight had no purchase.

Footsteps - his own - mingled with the sound of running water. The ground was solid rock, the walls smooth and cold and close. Tom had to keep his arms tight to his body to avoid them scraping either side of the narrow passage.

Ahead, the beam fanned out to light the smooth rock panelling the tunnel.

He clutched the stone heart in his right hand, its power to shift his world from the present to the tangled emotions of his past both terrifying and delicious.

He understood now that he was no ordinary boy. In what way he was special, Tom could not be certain. Was he really part of the family in his head? He brought his fist into the light, uncurled his fingers, looked at the pendant and tried to conjure the memory he knew he had of this place. It was there in his racing heart, the sweat on his forehead, the pull of fear tugging at his legs to slow him down. He was frightened. No! Terrified. If the ruin above Creggan was his home, this place was his Hell. Dredging his mind for a map, for some idea of what lay ahead, brought nothing but fear.

His pace began to drag, the soles of his feet one long scuffling sound followed by another. When his memory failed to deliver the information he needed, he tried logic and deduction. He quickly dismissed claustrophobia, natural caution, and fear of the dark. Trying to see through the cloud of emotion, he recalled his visions with dispassionate analysis, but still his feet scraped and dragged.

This was His place. This is where they went to learn.

They have to learn!

This is where *He* took his mother. Tess. The thought of it kindled his anger, muffled his fear. Whatever lay ahead gouged at a dormant and diseased lump stirring slowly in his soul. This is where the chairs were. The home of his pain. This was *His* lair.

He knew all this, but still the memory refused to crawl from under its rock.

Ahead, the tunnel walls fanned out and vanished. Tom paused on a half-dragged foot and turned his head from side to side. He removed the torch and held it before him with his left hand, but the beam disappeared to a black hole. He shone it on the floor, noting the undisturbed dust of passing years, pushed the light out and up, sweeping it left and right to take in the chamber he was about to enter. And he felt it then, too. A sense of openness - a blind man with one foot over the edge of a cliff.

That foot scraped forward and he stepped into the cave.

Pushing the torch ahead of him, he sensed something strange about the quality of the darkness beyond the beam. Pointing the torch to the side as he peered ahead, the void did not seem as black as it did when the glare had reflected into his eyes. He cupped the glass with his hand, smothering the light, but the cavern became brighter, instead of blacker. With trembling fingers, he twisted the top and killed the beam. Second by second, the darkness drifted away to reveal a continuous wash of light that seemed to come from the walls, the floor, the ceiling and even the very air itself. It was everywhere and yet came from nowhere at all.

He moved forward, his feet still dragging, the loathing for the place tugging on his back. But the light brought with it a kindling of the memory he searched for. He looked around and saw a wooden table against the wall to his right, dust an inch thick. Something scurried to his left. It was so close that when he swivelled his head, he was surprised to see nothing. There was nowhere for the creature to hide, but no matter how hard he stared, the animal remained invisible. More curious than frightened by some imaginary ghost rat, Tom continued the scan.

To the left of the table, covering an area of wall stretching over thirty feet long, was a home-made bookcase complete with an array of ancient volumes. He picked one at random and opened it. The pages were blank. He tried another and it too was empty. He flicked from cover to cover, felt the dust fill the air as he dislodged volume after volume, the roughness of thick fabric, the heft of each tome in his hands.

The books stretched upwards to the ceiling ten feet above. He climbed a shelf and stretched higher, knocking the objects and clouds of dust as he swept his hand over the top shelf, grabbing another as he tumbled backwards to the book-strewn floor. Lying there, he looked at the prize in his hand, felt the insane knowledge of what he was going to discover as he opened it and saw the empty pages turn and turn and turn. Staggering to his feet, Tom looked around at the rest of the space and caught his breath.

He had expected to see it, but when he did, the insanity of keeping a thousand books of nothing faded to the background and he almost vomited on the spot.

Stumbling over the scattered remains from the dislodged shelves, he walked forward in a bemused and terrified daze. A small archway led into another chamber from the wall opposite the bookshelves and there he saw what had to be there. He craned his neck as he walked. Water flowed, the sound a constant thunder in the echo-chamber of his head.

He couldn't actually see them at first, but that did not ease the grip the image had on him as he closed the distance between him and his nightmare. What he did see was a small pool, surrounded by a lip of rock. He remembered it then as if he was now walking towards it beside Tess, knowing what was to happen next. He would soon see the opening at the base of the artificial pond, the water gushing from the wall at one end, filling the pool and breaking through the gap to continue its journey out the mountain, past the cottage and into the sea. He could see none of this but knew it just the same.

And then he was there, standing in the archway looking at the strange high-backed chairs and the buzzing in his head pushed him to his knees and threatened to give him what he thought he wanted - memories.

TWENTY FOUR

Tom knelt in the dust, his right hand still clutching his precious stone, together with the left, pressing his temples in an effort to stop his head exploding. Every fact remembered came with a tortuous sizzle and pop as though its courier had just been zapped by an Insectacutor in his skull. Protecting his sanity, something inside the boy tried to shut the horrors out. Undeterred, the Tom struggling to know, drifted upright and slept-walked towards the pool. One after the other, his feet stepped over the lip, plunging ankle-deep into the freezing water. His dream seemed to catch his actions then, merging with them to form a powerful mix of senses that placed him back in time as though he was there.

And he was there.

In the real world he sat in a green-slimed and rotten seat, but behind closed eyes that same object had the clean lines of an electric chair He looked at the girl seated to his right, her grim face returning the look with a smile and a bite of her bottom lip. At the same time, in the present world - the real world - as Tom rested the back of his neck on the rusted cradle, he was alone, Tess a memory as clear as any moment lived in the present.

Feet sodden in the crystal Highland spring, the straps at the wrists, his waist and ankles seemed to fasten themselves. His head pushed back into its place of pain and he waited for the buzzing. He waited for the buzzing to grow and roil and swarm through his body.

He looked for Silas then. *Silas. Silas. Silas.*

George Silas.

The man. The tormentor.

And there he was. Sitting in front of them.

Tom and Tess.

And then he heard her. His mother. 'Tom! Tom!'

Silas smiled. 'It's up to you, boy. Her pain is yours to take away.'

Tom remembered the crackle of jagged light leap from the rod, the stench of burning flesh, his mother's limp body in Silas' arms. He was using her to get them to do what he wanted.

'Look at your sister. Feel her strength. Use it.'

Tom could not block the screams from his head, could not resist the urge to struggle against the straps binding him ever tighter to the seat of terror.

And then the circle of hands. Tess' love flowing from his right and the cold brutality of Silas crushing him from the left.

Once more the buzzing nodes bombed him with sound, pictures, facts.

Again the bright ball of light streaked across the unknown sky. Two naked and pink babies. A hideous creature, Silas, scooping the children in his arms and carrying them over hill and stream to a wild and beautiful place he recognised as Creggan. But in this Creggan there was no cottage and no ruin.

And suddenly it was there, built in the blink between two memories. A grim stone edifice that kept the weather out and the cold in. The babies turned to toddlers then and the toddlers were Tom and Tess.

And now there was a woman.

Their mother.

Laughing and singing. The cottage grew warm – became a home. This period - the children alone with their mother - seemed to stretch for years and Tom caught a glimpse of a life without Silas. Happy, loving, carefree.

And then *He* returned. The boat, the supplies, the pain.

A billion facts nipped at Tom's head and ripped through his body like a frenzied infestation. They buzzed through his fingers and he saw into Silas's thoughts mingling with his the younger Tom's and Tess'.

He saw a huge castle. High on black rock. Sombre children praying, their dark faces a curious mix of contentment and dread. And then there were thousands of voices, millions of thoughts, billions of facts ravaging his mind. The cradle at his neck seemed to hiss with the searing heat on his flesh.

Somewhere his mother cried out. 'Tom. Tom.'

Tess' grip slackened on his. The equations, the obscure names, the references to strangers and places unknown, slowed from a torrent to a trickle and then to a stop.

Tom opened his eyes, knowing this time that what he had experienced was not a present reality, but a memory as vivid as the experience itself.

Still, he heard his name. It bounced on the walls, his mother crying out in fear and anguish. This time, he knew where to look. Jumping from the seat, he splashed through the pool and ran into the main chamber, turning immediately to his left. Another arch led into a cave so small that he had to crouch to enter it.

And there she was. His mother, looking at him, her rescuer, her son. She tried to smile through silent tears.

She opened her arms and Tom fell on her, his emotions treasured pain he wanted to suffer - a mixture of happiness that he was with her at last and fear and anger for how she was treated.

He wrapped his arms around her and crumpled to a pile of misery when he felt nothing but empty, cold air and the cruel realisation that his mind was still determined to trick him whenever it could.

Tom lay in abject isolation. The image had caught up with reason and now all he saw was a chain fastened to a wall, a single, empty manacle lying rusted on the floor.

As he lay there, tears flowing freely, he heard his mother call again, but this time he did not move. It was another trick. She was not there. The dust had gathered undisturbed for years - the place no more than a mausoleum for his ghoulish memories. The most he could hope for was to use the cavern as a painful forum in which to rebuild his notion of self. Who he was.

Still, once more the light surrounding him changed. It dimmed as his name drifted on a glob of light as bright as the sun. It hissed and popped as it neared. 'Tom? Tom!'

And soon he could see little beyond the sun until Katriana moved the lamp from in front, to her side and they stood in complete darkness again, wrapped in a small bubble of white light.

TWENTY FIVE

'Oh my God.'

Katriana swung the lamp slowly from side to side. It was obvious from her wide-eyed expression and hesitant movements that she was frightened, but still she stood her ground. She had, after all, braved the entry to the cave on her own and now her fear was as much for Tom's safety and sanity as for her own.

Tom could not see what she could but sensed what she felt.

The boy had been lying in total darkness. He jumped to his feet as she approached and now stood blinking rapidly as he stared in turns at the lamp and then at the girl. His face, his clothes, his matted hair were coloured cremation-grey. His shoes and lower legs were sopping, blobs of congealed dust clumping the fabric and the stone floor he stood on.

It was his face. Though, that shocked Katriana. Even in the super-white light of the gas lamp, despite the ashen make-up trying to fake the look, the girl could see that Tom's real skin was the colour of death.

'There's no-one here,' whispered Tom, as if that explained everything. Made it safe.

She stretched a hand, her eyes glancing at the rusted chain hanging from the wall. Tom reached out, accepting her help. He felt her flinch as they connected and saw her face twist as she resisted the urge to pull back. But when nothing happened, no ghoulish pictures invaded her head, she gripped him tightly and pulled him to her and away from the open cell.

They walked through the large cavern past the strange bookcase, the pile of empty books he'd thrown to the floor. He had an urge to look again, but Katriana's pace did not slow and he was too weak, too emotionally battered to resist. That changed when he saw a single, loose-bound volume lying on the ground beneath the table. Something lurched inside Tom. He recognised the object as surely as he had the heart stone. It too had belonged to his mother. He wrenched himself from Katriana's grasp and stooped to pick it up.

Katriana was about to snap at him when she saw his fevered hands fumble the object with reverential fear.

'I know this,' he whispered and then commanded. 'The lamp.'

Katriana looked towards the exit tunnel and then at the blackness of the cave beyond the reach of their bubble of light. She shivered, but was infected by Tom's sudden excitement. She placed the lamp on the table and drew herself to the boy's side as he laid the book flat on the dusty top.

'My mother. It was hers.'

Katriana stiffened. 'Your mother? How...?'

But her words trailed away. Their shared vision of the family gathering during the séance was still strong. So too, was the sense of love and devotion between the woman and Tom.

And this was her diary?

Katriana suspected that Tom's need for a family made him over-react to the vision she had conjured, but there was no doubting that he had found the cave exactly where he'd looked for it. And now the diary. Could it really be hers?

The sense of evil in the cave was difficult to fight, but if something was going to attack them, then surely it would have done so already.

Tom caressed the cover. Given his earlier experience with the bookcase, he feared the pages would be as blank as those in that strange collection, but when he flicked through the bundle in his hands, he saw immediately that he was wrong.

'It's the same paper,' Katriana whispered. Both Tom and the girl pictured the woman scribbling happily on the beach before her world turned to pain.

To call the bundle a book was a stretch. Rough, yellow paper scratched over with black ink kept together by a loose leather cover, crackled in his hands and threw dust in the air. Katriana sneezed. The paper was so dry that Tom worried the thing might disintegrate with each tiny movement. He placed the pile flat on the table and turned the front cover with two hands as though he was a librarian entrusted with a first-edition bible. The heart in his hand touched his mother's words for the first time in years and he gasped at the sight of her neat and artful writing. Centred, and still bold despite years of neglect, she had written:

The Private Journal of Kathleen Henderson 1852-

The final date was incomplete and Tom ignored the obvious implication. In his world nothing was obvious.

Some of the entries were unreadable but whole passages survived intact, the writing a flourish of swirls and loops waltzing through her life.

The first complete sentences were close to the beginning:

Another good night. Please God let her live.

And two pages on:

Her cough's back. Blood and phlegm. She looks so frail.

It was another ten pages before he read the following:

A part of me feels guilty for wanting Mither back - for missing her so. God has taken her pain away. I should rejoice, says Father James. I must be a selfish woman because I cannot see beyond the loss of her.

Various partial entries talked about the funeral and it was obvious to Tom and Katriana that the woman was alone in the world. She had looked after her mother for so long that she had no life of her own. A woman before her time, before the girl in her had lived its span.

There was a long period when little was written before the journal took another turn:

Father James has a job for me. I know little of the case, but he urges me to leave for Arran immediately. It's so far away.

T*he bailiff has given me two days to leave the house. Mither was a master at hiding our debt. I had no idea.*

Mr Silas called. Poor man is wretched. He was disfigured badly trying to rescue his wife from a fire. He is left with two bairns. I must help.

Tom stiffened, drew a gasp of foetid and dusty air. He knew exactly who those babies were and the implications were devastating on so many levels that his head began to spin.

He tightened his grip on the stone and willed the soft embrace of his mother to enfold him, to protect him from this new and vile truth.

But the embrace did not appear and the truth closed and crushed and crumpled the carefully constructed world that centred on the love of his mother. And the truth was that she wasn't.

She wasn't his mother, but a lost soul lured to the aid of a poor man whose need was greater than hers.

A poor unfortunate, crippled and heroic; George Silas.

TWENTY SIX

Katriana understood the effect those words had on Tom. She covered his hand with hers and noticed the stone. 'What's that?' she asked.

'It's my moth....' He paused and choked back the word *mother.* 'It's hers.' He nodded to the journal as Katriana brought the heart close to the lamp. 'It's so beautiful,' she whispered and passed it back to the boy.

They were about to return to the journal when the sound of a small animal, similar to the one Tom heard earlier, echoed through the chamber. This time, the scurrying came from a point to their left by the books. Katriana and Tom both jumped as a blur of fur zipped along the top of a line of books on the middle shelf. This time the rat, because that's what it was, was visible and huge. Katriana shivered. 'We should leave. We can read the journal in the cottage. This place gives me the jeebies.'

Staring after the rat, she seemed to see the books for the first time. Despite her call to leave, she stooped to the floor and retrieved a leather-bound volume.

'They're all blank,' said Tom.

Katriana looked down at a random page. 'No they're not,' she replied. 'Who would keep a stack of blank books?'

Curious, Tom looked at the sample she had tilted towards him. Sure enough, Katriana seemed to have stumbled on the only volume that wasn't actually blank.

'What is it?' he asked.

'Maths, I think. Or maybe physics. Lots of formulae anyway.' She passed the book to Tom and rummaged at her feet for another. Tom glanced at the pages in his hand and marvelled at the tiny writing cramming every inch of clear space in a complex pattern of gobbledygook.

Although, it wasn't gobbledygook. Not to him.

'This is a calculation for skin conduction. Transdermal information flow.'

Katriana looked up from her acquisition and raised an eyebrow. 'Of course it is.'

Despite themselves they both smiled, but Tom was drawn to the second book in her hand. It too was full of writing. He picked another from the floor and another from the shelves. Time after time he got the same result. Full. Not a blank page among them. Science. Mathematics. Politics. History. Anatomy. Nanotech. And time after time, the information contained was akin to common sense once Tom read a piece to himself, no matter how obscure or how complex the subject.

'These were all empty. All of them.'

Katriana looked at Tom suspiciously. 'You mean like magic ink,' she quipped.

'No, I'm serious. This means something.'

'It means something alright, but not to me.' She looked at the spines lining the shelves and added. 'How come they're in such good condition? This is ancient. They should have rotted or been eaten by Basil and his friends.'

'Basil?' Tom asked.

'The rat.'

'Oh right. I see.' But, of course, he didn't see at all. Still, those words, *I see,* planted a notion in the boy's mind that would have seemed wild to a normal person and yet, made immediate and weird sense to Tom.

'Put out the lamp,' he said.

Katriana was unimpressed by Tom's assumption that she would obey his order and she said without thinking, 'Put it out yourself.'

And he did, much to Katriana's alarm. He walked to the table, reached out as Katriana fumbled her warning not to, and closed the knurled valve until the hiss turned to a spluttering, popping halt and the cave plunged to darkness.

'Ahhh!' Katriana screamed.

'Quiet. There's no-one here. It's all right.'

'You're a lunatic, Tom. Put it back on.'

Tom's answer was unexpected. 'Wow,' he said - and then said it again. 'Wow!'

When the light died, Tom saw nothing but a dark void unlike any darkness experienced on the surface above. It was as if someone had painted his eyeballs black. But second by second, that strange, all embracing light lifted his surroundings from obscurity and brought the cavern into sharp focus.

The table, the journal opened to the page he had left it at, the words, *George Silas* poisoning the purity of its writer's intentions. He glanced at the book in his hand and noted that it too was full of detailed ink.

Katriana stood between the pile on the floor and the wall of books. She was misshapen; her edges blurred as though a living painting whose artist had not quite decided where to put her. She cursed Tom for his stupidity and Tom was surprised to note that the sound came from a point to the left of her body. As soon as she spoke however, the body jerked sideways to match the location of her voice. Now though, her shape was more indistinct, its substance fading like a departing ghost. The girl stumbled over the books, her image performing an approximation of the action before blurring to a wispy representation of her form sprawled in the general area before him.

'Help me, Tom,' she cried. And the shape firmed a little to its right.

Tom reached down. 'Give me your hand,' he said.

This time, she did not seem to mind the order. A smoky and blurred arm swiped the air and Tom felt the girl's warm fingers brush his. They met and grasped and Tom pulled an angry girl to her feet.

'What are you playing at?' she spat.'

'I can see,' Tom said.

Katriana's face sharpened in front of his as her breath brushed his lips. He pocketed the heart, held her hand and circled her waist to comfort her.

'Well, maybe *see* isn't the right word. Maybe the word should be *remember!*'

TWENTY SEVEN

'Please, Katriana. Trust me.'

Tom felt the girl shaking and he wasn't quite sure how much of that was from anger and how much of it was from the shock she received by being plunged into darkness. He led her to the table, her feet stuttering on quaking limbs through the unseen cave.

'I'm going to let you go. I have to light the lamp. Here,' he said. 'Put your hands on the tabletop.' She did and Tom turned the valve and heard the satisfying hiss.

Katriana spoke, her voice still shaking. A fraction calmer. 'The red button. Press it.' Tom did so and a spark inside the chamber fired the gas to a bright glow that blinded him. As Tom rubbed his eyes clear of the molten blobs that came and went with each blink, Katriana flew at him.

'You moron.' She clenched her fist and curved a punch on his right shoulder so that he almost dropped the lamp. Her temper threw another blow, this time an open-handed slap to his left cheek.

'Owh!'

'What do you think, Pea-Brain? Scare the wee lassie, is it?'

Tom considered switching off the lamp again to get her under control, but decided against it as blow after blow caused him to back away.

'It wasn't that, Katriana. I'm serious. I can sort of see in the dark.'

The words finally found their mark and Katriana stopped her advance on him.

'That's impossible,' she said.

'I know.'

He moved sideways, keeping beyond her reach, and replaced the lamp on the table.

'I saw it when I came into the cave. That's why you found me in the dark. To me it wasn't. Dark, I mean.'

Tom warmed to the notion as one deduction followed another.

'Although, I don't think I see in the dark at all,' he mused.

'Tom, you make less sense every minute I talk to you.'

Tom then had an idea.

'Hang on. I want to try something.'

'Touch the lamp and I kill you.'

Tom ignored her and scanned the cave, noting again where everything was. For the moment, his sense of loss and confusion, the hatred he felt for Silas, the contradiction of time-scales and the curse of his irrational emotions faded with the excitement of this extraordinary discovery. He focused on the location of the table, the heap of books on the floor, the strange library, the far archways leading to the pool and to the prison room.

He visualised the dimensions, the positioning of the walls, scanned the floor ahead for anything he might trip over.

He then closed his eyes. Scrunched them tight.

Katriana, her dislike of the place urging her to flee, was irritated and confused.

'If you don't stop playing games, I'm leaving you here.'

Tom ignored her. He was trying to picture the space as it was before he closed his eyes. He walked forward, resisting the need to raise his arms in a parody of blind-man's-buff.

At first he was quite confident, taking six long strides across the empty floor but soon his steps slowed and shortened. He thought himself close to the far wall, but what if he had strayed to the right? His feet dragged, toes prodding the air and tapping the floor like a white stick. He wished he'd paid more attention to what was beyond the straight line from the table to the opening he blundered towards.

He stopped, listening to the water tinkling around the chair legs dead ahead. He was still on target.

'This proves nothing. Anyone can do that.'

The words seemed to slap him in the back and he stumbled forward. She was right. Close your eyes and you can walk around chairs, sofas and even well-behaved dogs for a few seconds.

This thought stumbled through his head as he blundered across the room, his arms now twirling to keep his balance, his eyes threatening to spring open.

And then he saw everything. Just like that!

Lids still firmly shut, that all-embracing strange light reappeared and Tom saw the entrance to the chair-chamber two steps ahead. He caught his balance and walked in.

At his back, Katriana had started another round of berating him when she stopped suddenly and said. 'You've got your eyes open.'

'Shh,' said Tom.

He quickened his step, walked through the archway, and heard Katriana run lightly towards him at his back, the strengthening hiss of the lamp.

She passed close to his side as he squatted by the pool scooping a handful of water to his lips. He sensed the girl standing beside him as he turned, felt the heat of her and then saw her. She was indistinct - wispy smoke approximating her shape, her position, her movements. Katriana's face, however, was eerily beautiful, her long black hair wafting gently with each shift in her position.

She was staring at him now and Tom felt her studying his closed eyes as he moved.

Forgetting, for an instant, the terrible setting, the torture-chamber of his childhood, the boy felt invincible. He could see in the dark! A rush of adrenalin lifted his spirits and he had a sudden and uncontrollable urge to show off. He reached out and, with uncanny accuracy, took the lamp from Katriana, placed it on the floor, grasped her smoky hands in his and, eyes still closed, hummed his best orchestral waltz. He whisked her around the chamber in a dance of surreal and short-lived joy.

'You really can see,' she said. She held her head back, watching him, noting his closed eyes, the way he turned, this way and that, to navigate the obstacles, steer clear of the walls, the table, the books.

Katriana stopped and Tom's temporary madness subsided, the rush of his new-found skill a mere link in the tangled chain of his life.

He opened his eyes and blinked at the strange sensation of seeing the cavern much as he did with them closed. The quality of the light was different, the lamp dominating everything, pushing much of the cave into darkness beyond its immediate sphere, shadows springing into existence where there were none seconds before.

'It's in my head,' Tom said. 'A memory.'

'Like a map?' asked Katriana.

'Perhaps; but detailed. It moves when I move, when I look around.' Tom was excited, warming to his new understanding. He rushed over to the books and plucked one from a middle shelf. Opening it at a random place, he saw the small writing, the mathematical squiggles. 'And this,' he said showing her the writing as though it was a new language he had just discovered. 'The pages were blank because I'd never looked between the covers before. I had nothing to recall.'

'What about me? You saw me, didn't you?'

'Sort of. I pictured where I thought you were, but it was sometimes wrong. Your voice would be in the wrong place.'

Tom's excitement faded. He looked around and put the chamber back in context. No discovery, no matter how exciting, how close it brought him to learning who he was, would shake the horror of this place from his soul. His mood crashed and, even though he knew that the woman he thought of as his mother wasn't, the sense of loss for his family, the impotence of knowing that he was helpless to stop what had happened in another time, and the certainty that he was alone, crushed him like falling earth to a grave.

'Who am I?' Tom whispered.

But Katriana shook her head and answered with a question of her own. 'No, Tom – Not *who,* but, *what* are you?'

TWENTY EIGHT

Getting Tom to leave the cavern was difficult, but when Katriana agreed to help him take a handful of books back to the cottage, he reluctantly agreed. It was not that he wanted to stay. He hated the place as much as, and more, than Katriana. But things were happening. No matter how it hurt, he had to continue forward and this place, these things, the books, they were clues. He needed to study them all.

Outside, the unfettered air cleansed his lungs like iced water flushing phlegm. He could taste the sweet night, feel its cold sting in his chest. Pushing down on the metal stirrup, Tom sealed the entrance. It closed as quietly as it had opened.

Returning to the cottage, Katriana checked on her father while Tom piled their catch on the coffee table and spread the journal beside it.

He looked at the title again and thought of the woman sitting on the beach. He could not shake the feeling that she was his mother, but he wondered then about the boy. Until now he had given in to the impossible notion that the Tom in his visions and the boy buried in his head were one and the same person. Away from the source - the emotional maelstrom surrounding the ruin and the cave - he allowed other, less fanciful possibilities, to wander his thoughts. Perhaps Katriana was right. Perhaps he was sensitive to a tragedy imprinted on the fabric of this enigmatic place. Perhaps too, the powerful senses of love and hate were illusions brought on by his need to belong. And then there was the possibility that there was indeed a connection between him and the long-dead family, a connection as simple as genetic ancestry or as spiritual as reincarnation.

Could the memories he experienced be somehow passed from generation to generation?

As he pondered this question, Katriana called to him from the other room. 'Tom! Quick!'

When he saw Calum, Tom understood the panic in her voice. The man was soaking wet, swaying his head from side to side as if he was having a slow-motion fit. The cover was pulled aside and the lamp close to his leg.

'My God,' Tom said and then regretted it immediately when he saw the concern on Katriana's face.

Calum's injured limb was not discoloured, it was dipped in black ink, dabbed by splashes of pussy green.

'He's been getting worse since you left. I had to find you. I don't care what happens now. We've got to get help.'

Tom fought back the words *about time too* and said instead, 'I'll get ready.'

Remarkably, Katriana did not jump at the offer. '

'No.'

She was emphatic. 'You're confused, Tom. Ill. The bump on the head. The waking dreams.'

Tom was sure she meant hallucinations.

'If that's gangrene, he could die,' he told her.

'And if you get lost in the dark, he doesn't get the help he needs.'

Tom thought of the map of the cavern in his head. Could he find his way from Creggan to Lochranza?

No, Katriana was right. Light would dawn in a few hours. He should go then.

Katriana re-covered her father and wrung a cool cloth into a basin at the side of the bed. She placed it across his forehead and sat down holding his hand, ignoring Tom completely.

Tom placed a hand on her shoulder. 'If you need me, shout.'

The girl nodded tearfully, her eyes fixed forward as though in a trance.

Tom left and retook his position on the settee.

Once he spied the journal, Calum's injury was set aside and he settled down to read.

*

Kathleen Henderson, all those years ago, moved to Arran to

look after George Silas' children. He was a strange man. She could not tell at first if his dismissive manner and reclusive lifestyle were due to his injuries. He was in constant pain and the carer in her tried to comfort him with small kindnesses. At first he brushed these aside, commanding her not to fuss, but soon Kathleen's attempts to engage with the man brought harsh words and a flash of temper that scared her enough to quell her natural sympathies. She retreated to the care of the children and found in them a happiness she thought belonged to others. To her horror the children were not even named. Silas referred to them as *him* and *her* until the woman christened them Thomas and Tessa.

In the early years, the bizarre man left them for months at a time, bringing with him, on each return, a compilation of equipment that Kathleen could not understand. She began to fear that the demented creature was undertaking Satan's work. This expression, especially the word *Satan*, caused Tom to pause. He was terrified by the notion and for some reason thought of the children he had glimpsed in the dark castle, praying to someone or something hidden from his mind. He was certain that Kathleen's comment was no more than a euphemism for work that she suspected as evil, but this did not stop Tom shaking, or sweat beading his forehead, as the word *Satan* exploded in his mind. And behind that word, the sense and sounds of a billion souls writhing in unknown graves, screaming for help.

And to Tom, it seemed as if the very prayer they screamed flew at him and for a mad fleeting instant, the tortured souls were turned his way and yelled as one, 'Help us! Help us die. Please help us die!'

TWENTY NINE

If Tom had been left alone with the cry of humanity in his head, he might have gone mad. Indeed, he thought he may already have done so. He had almost vomited when it happened and it took all his strength not to scream for help of his own. But who would help him? Katriana and her father had their problems too.

No! Tom had to face his demons alone. He had been so focused on trying to find out who he was and how he was connected to Creggan's past that the boy stumbled from one discovery to another with little control over what happened and when. The vision on the boat and his first sighting of Kathleen happened with no obvious input from him, but the séance, his search for the hidden ramp, the pendant, the strange and realistic map of the cavern in his head - all of these were linked to actions he had initiated. Even the horrific screams had been triggered, it seemed, by the journal he'd been reading.

He may be mad, but the cave and the chairs and the pendant were real. The journal and the books, puzzle-pieces clicking clean and crisp with each new insight.

He refused to run. The problem was part of him and running would surely be for life. He would grasp the challenge tight to his chest and charge.

He closed his eyes and recalled the faces and their cries for help. There was nothing special about the people he'd seen. Men, women and children of every age and race howled in anguish, all of them looking his way, all of them, billions it seemed, somehow able to occupy the tiny space in his head and yet still maintain an impression of individuality. It had all happened so fast that Tom could not fathom this contradiction. A conglomerate of lonely souls. He could remember no more than four glimpsed faces now - A girl, roughly fourteen years old, her hair dyed yellow, her bright white shirt incongruously set against the twisted skin of her face, her expression distorting otherwise model good looks. A man, white-haired, but fit in body, now withering and bent in a brief moment of accelerated degeneration, his head turned towards Tom from a kneeling position, pleading for death. A young boy, about five-years-old, his face aged by pain, tears and snot surrounding the large cavern of his mouth as he bawled in agony. And finally a black woman, young, brilliant white teeth made for smiling, now gritted between stretched and parched lips as her eyes flared red with agony and she too joined the chorus pleading for Tom's help. For Tom to help them die.

He paraded them, one after the other, before his inner eye. In doing so, he felt their desperation.

He tried to see beyond, to their surroundings, but could not. In his mind they were a populace of individuals, but there were so many of them that no place on Earth could hold them in anything but large groups. Could this be no more than a hellish nightmare? A place where sense and nonsense slept like mismatched lovers. Tom possessed a strange ability to channel things, abnormal things, through his mind. This he accepted.

That did not mean, though, that he did not experience normal things too. He ate, breathed, walked and talked like everyone else. Why not nightmares? The thought was vaguely comforting.

He was saved from his self destructive courage by another scream, this time from the patient and his daughter next door. Tom jumped to his feet and bolted to their aid.

Running into the room, he found Katriana wrapping her arms around her father's shoulders, fighting to keep her grip as he thrashed from side to side. As Tom took in the scene, the man suddenly sat up and his legs swung over the side of the bed. The boy instinctively dived for them, wincing at the thought of the giant's bulk bearing down on the bloated and black limb.

Calum's eyes were bloodshot, staring straight to the front wherever his head pointed. Despite the man's strength, Tom managed to pin his feet to the bed as Katriana shushed him as though he were a massive, teething baby.

By the time his seizure ended, Tom was in no doubt what had to be done and for once he and the girl agreed.

Leaving her father's side for no more than two minutes, Katriana reminded Tom to follow the path without deviating. It was still dark, but dawn was on its way. She tipped out a small sack, stuffed the torch in his hand, her own waterproof jacket inside the sack and opened the door as if he had been an unwelcome guest at an over-long party.

'It's less than five miles. The weather looks good. Even with the hill you should be there in two, maybe three hours.'

She glanced behind her, anxious to get back to her father. Tom half-smiled and turned to go, the small sack slung casually over his left shoulder. Katriana swung the door closed and then paused. They had been moving so fast since the decision was made that this two-second interlude seemed like the still calm of a painted dream.

In that beat, their eyes met, their half-formed smiles locked and then finally, and slowly, the door closed between them.

Tom stood looking at the darkened green wood, blinked away the feelings of dread and loss, turned on his heels and sprinted towards the path.

*

A faint, pale-blue wash tinged the ruffled hills across the sea. With the brightness of the cottage gone and the smudge of light on the horizon, Tom could see enough to move steadily along the path without the torch. Once moving, the surge of adrenalin flooding his system gave him a rush of energy that pushed back the utter exhaustion that should have slowed him down.

The half-slung sack now squarely in its proper place over both shoulders, he pummelled hard with one leg and then another, storming the initial incline as though pursued by relentless hunters. Slowing briefly to look at the ruin passing to his left and the rocks hiding the cave, he recovered his pace with perfect rhythm. Sweat on his back, he drove the path as it swung right and levelled out, cutting at an angle along the hill. Below and to his right, the far undulating horizon turned a light pink and a gentle breeze blew over the water and up the hill. It cooled his face as he watched the land slip slowly beneath him. First the cottage and then the enormous boulders with their miniature caves and hidden graves. And then the sloping greenery disappeared over what he assumed was the birthing cliff for his present life. In another time, he would have scouted the area to look for a clue to how he got there, but that seemed unimportant now.

It was almost light by the time the path rounded the dip between the hill he was on and the next. The pink line had now stained the underside of high clouds and the sky became a beautiful roof of spectacular red light.

Curving over the saddle, the path started its slow descent into the glen. To his left, and still in shadow, a grey tarmac road roped along the bottom of the hill opposite. A bright yellow car pushed its headlights and its driver towards a new day.

Running beside a stream, the path disappeared to mud and then the mud disappeared to path. He slithered and stumbled and ran and ran.

And as the scorched sky blued and brightened, he saw a tiny gathering of houses and then another. He saw the road again, back from an excursion hidden by trees, bright grey now, zooming through green fields as the glen widened towards the sea. He was in another world. A world of people, of transport, of comfort and help.

Stopping for nothing, he pumped his arms and continued down the hill and entered the village of Lochranza.

THIRTY

Lochranza, small, beautiful, sitting quietly at the top of the island. To Tom's right, in the east and hidden by a small grassy mountain, the sleepy sea held Creggan's coast and Ayrshire's apart. Directly in front as he descended a narrow track, water spilled inland to a tiny loch marking Arran's north east corner. The main part of the village lay to its left; a straggle of buildings strung out on the far side of the road as it bordered the loch.

Stumbling on an isolated house, the boy wasted precious minutes battering on the door. He yelled through the letterbox, frustrated by the telephone sitting on a three-legged table in the hallway. He briefly considered breaking in but, so close to Lochranza proper, he reluctantly ran on. When at last his feet slapped on tarmac, Tom paused and bent double, his hands flat on his thighs and breathing hard.

The road ran left to the village and straight on to skirt the right side of the loch to a dead end. A quiet line of houses overlooked the tranquil water. In another life, Tom might have found the setting idyllic but at that moment there was nothing familiar about the place.

The tiny hamlet was close, the line of houses ahead closer still. He straightened up, drew a breath, and as he steeled himself to run again, a noisy clattering beat shredded the soft dawn behind him. He whirled in fright to face the sound.

A yellow helicopter swooped fast and low through the glen. It roared to his left, the words, *Royal Air Force Rescue,* stencilled on its hide, its nose tilted forward as though sniffing the earth. Kneeling at a large square opening in the fuselage, a crewman studied the ground as the machine flared up close to the near-edge of the village.

The engine roared, grass and trees shook and the Sea King

paused before settling slowly onto a clearing by the road. Beyond the chopper, a small ruin of a castle, a quiet icon of Scottish heritage overlooked the busy scene. Two machines built for war doing time on community service.

As the winch-man talked the pilot down, Tom noticed a clutch of vehicles clustered nearby. Land Rovers and cars. And people too. Men and women with rucksacks, police in uniform. Tom knew what he had to do. Turning left, he skirted the top of the loch, turned right at the main road, and ran towards the gathering.

*

No-one paid attention to the boy entering the arena. The chopper blades had stopped, drooped, tired and silent. Two crew members poked around a hanging panel and another, the pilot, Tom assumed, dressed in a one-piece olive-green uniform with cloth wings on his chest, talked to a policeman. A group of rescuers, radio aerials protruding from heavy rucksacks, hunched over the bonnet of a Land Rover, inspecting a map spread on its blue-grey surface.

Beside them, a magnetic white board stood against the windscreen of another vehicle. Two photographs topped a list of radio call-signs and names.

The photographs stopped Tom, dead.

Minutes before, when he had first seen what was obviously a search operation, the boy had silently thanked his luck. Stumbling so quickly on the people sent to find Katriana and her father was more than he could have hoped for. The chopper could be at Creggan in ten minutes and a hospital soon after. But now he looked at the images in confusion. He stared and stared at them.

Two pictures, two people and although neither were what he expected, he knew them both. They had been scanned from originals, computer-enhanced to remove scratches, isolate each subject. Despite their apparent ancient origins, the figures were instantly recognisable. He stood wide-eyed beside the men briefing over the Land Rover's bonnet.

The pictures had been old - very old. But the likeness was remarkable, even in sepia tones. A faded yellow wash jaundiced the skin and severe stares indicated that the models had *sat long enough, thank you.*

He moved closer, bumping lightly against a man listening to the huddled brief. The leader addressed the group in short crisp sentences.

'They're likely to be confused. Might even resist your help...'

The voice trailed away and the rescuer he had bumped against glanced casually over his shoulder at Tom.

Tom floated onward until he stood by the second vehicle. He reached over and took the photographs from the board, one in each hand. As he stared at the photo of himself, the man he'd brushed against took a glance at his own copy cupped in the palm of his hand. He looked from it to the boy and back again. He spoke softly, interrupting the team leader's talk. 'Donald. I think we need another plan.'

'What!?' came the indignant reply. But a moment later all eyes were on the boy standing no more than ten feet from their collective and confused centre. Tom was unaware of the attention building around him. He was preoccupied by the second image. There she was, in glorious sepia, her red hair hidden by low-tech photography. The girl in his vision, the girl he thought in a moment of madness might have been his sister from another time. Tess!

THIRTY ONE

Tom sat facing the open square of the chopper. The winch-man checked his lap-strap, gave him two yellow pieces of foam the size of pencil erasers and mimed plugging his ears. Tom nodded and squashed the buds home until the deafening noise was muffled. Still, the machine shook him to his bones. The surreal isolation enclosed him like a dream. The world of the ordinary he had just entered felt so strange - the muted fury of the blades scything the air in a never-ending circle, the smell of engine exhaust, the shimmering view, bright and square and filled with strangers. And everything bathed in the knowledge that, somewhere out there, his sister was as alive or dead as Schrödinger's cat.

Beside him, from the canvas seat to his right, Chief Inspector David Howard turned and gave Tom the thumbs up. They sat with their backs to the fuselage on the Sea King's port side.

Tom tried to smile but was too full of anticipation and worry to succeed. The engine screamed, grass and heather shook, rescuers outside dropped to one knee and averted their eyes. The ground and the people fell away, slid sideways beyond the opening and disappeared from sight.

Tom's excitement bubbled and he squirmed in his seat. He had told Howard about Katriana and her father. But no, he did not know where Tess was. He urged speed, impressed on him that Calum could die. The debrief was painfully slow and Tom was annoyed at the way the man had isolated him in a police van and talked to him alone and quietly as though he were a fragile child.

At last something seemed to twig inside the officer's mind and he had led Tom to the helicopter.

Now they were on their way.

Outside, the scenery slid sideways. The loch disappeared and the hill he had descended took its place. He saw in the thin line running up the slope, every step of his earlier journey to the village, but the pain of his run was replaced by an emotion he'd not expected and he blushed. In a few minutes he would see Katriana again. He would descend from the sky outside the cottage and she would be standing there, her long black hair flailing wildly in the down-draft. He would smile gently and they would load her father into the aircraft and somehow, he didn't yet know how, he would find a way to be close to her and to know her better.

They moved fast and within seconds broke beyond the point he knew would take them directly to Creggan. They passed it by in a blink and with each second Tom braced himself for the dramatic hand-brake turn that would swing them left, up and over the green summit.

But it never came.

Tom yelled to the winch-man's back, silhouetted as it was against the bright vibrating world outside.

'Over there!' he screamed, pointing to the tail end of the aircraft. The Inspector took the boy's hand and gently lowered it to his lap. He turned in his seat and placed his lips an inch from Tom's ear.

'Don't worry, Tom. They'll be fine.'

This only made things worse. How could they be fine? The helicopter was the quickest way to get help to them. They could be landing in thirty seconds. He should be on his way to see Katriana again. Instead they snuffled the ground fast and low towards the south of the Island. At his back, through a small window on the side of the aircraft, Tom saw with aching and twisted neck muscles, mountains of rock turn the bright dawn grey. Tearing at the buckle on his lap, he freed himself and lunged towards the open door. He grabbed the winch-man to get his attention.

And he succeeded.

Even through the earplugs, over and above the muted cacophony of the bone-shaker, he heard the man yell in fright. Safely cabled to the aircraft, the shock of contact spun him in one explosive move to confront Tom. The man grabbed him and pinned his arms to his side. He was gentle but strong. He pushed him back to his seat.

'It's OK, Tom. You're safe. We're taking you home.'

The crewman screamed this in his ear but with the furious noise, the isolating plugs and the insane vibration, Tom did not take in what he'd said at first. 'You've gone past them!' The boy's throat rasped as though his words were edged with roughened stone. The policeman at his side patted his head and said something like, 'There, there. Don't be frightened.'

And it was then that the crewman's use of the word *home* sunk in to Tom's frazzled brain. He slumped in his seat and Howard cupped his hand over Tom's.

He leaned over as the winch-man returned to his duties by the open door.

'Look, we're here.'

They were over a forest but Tom did not know what he was supposed to be looking at. All he could think of was Katriana and how he had let her down. A subtle depression snaked through the trees. It wound inland, away from the ring-road and the sea. A private road, obscured by overlapping branches, burrowed through the forest

And then he saw what they were headed for.

Two miles on, the trees cleared to circle a green manicured lawn. At its centre was an enormous, majestic baronial building that some would call a house and others, fixated by the crenellated walls, a fortress. It was as grey as a castle, as magnificent as a palace.

The Inspector squeezed Tom's hand and said something he couldn't hear.

The aircraft circled the house and then dropped gently to the lawn directly in centre-front.

Given the nod from the winch-man, Howard unlatched himself and then the boy. He had to tug on Tom to get him to move. Tom drifted to the opening and vaulted into the strange new world that was supposed to be home. When they had cleared the blades, the chopper lifted from the grey granite backdrop of the building, blasting their backs and whipping their hair to a frenzy of storm-lashed fronds. It disappeared exactly fifty eight minutes after he had first seen the thing thunder down the glen.

Together, man and boy, they watched the departing helicopter. Tom waited for it to bank left, to retrace the route they'd taken to get to this spot, but once more it ignored his will to budge. To his horror it kept on straight, running east over the hidden sea until it was nothing but a strange memory in his already warped mind.

Inspector Howard said something incoherent. The man tapped

him on the shoulder and Tom remembered then to remove the plugs. Turning to the house, he saw a single figure, a man, standing at the top junction of two curved sets of steps that mirrored each other like the edges of grey petals.

'Come on lad,' the Inspector said.

Tom ignored him. 'Why isn't the helicopter going to Creggan?'

The man was momentarily distracted as though the question had caught him off guard but then he smiled like a politician and said, 'We already had a police launch checking the cottage. They picked your friends up. They're going to be fine.'

Tom was disappointed and elated all at once. He had missed the chance of seeing Katriana's face when he arrived with help, but at least he'd kept his word and brought them to safety. He only wished that the policeman had explained earlier.

Putting an arm around his shoulder, Howard walked his catch towards the house. Tom shivered as the policeman said, 'You're home at last, lad. Home and safe.'

THIRTY TWO

In the sudden quiet of the early morning, Tom's mood lifted as he walked up the steps. Close by, a lone cuckoo claimed the morning and the waiting trees breathed the soft sigh of a wandering, fragrant breeze. Bright flowers seemed to suddenly line every border of the lawn and the grey house sparkled with windows and the promise of memories yet to be revealed. Memories of his forgotten childhood.

And yet, it wasn't forgotten. If this was home, what then of his Creggan dreams, Kathleen and Tess? Soon, he told himself on that slow walk up the stairs, soon he would know. Soon he would have peace. And soon, he hoped, Tess would be found and the craziness of the past days lain to rest at last. These were not real, conscious thoughts forming in his mind but rather a state of being, a reaction to hearing that Katriana was safe and that this was somehow home.

Somehow.

The schizophrenic bastion glowered over them, infecting Tom's mood with wild and extreme swings.

His slow climb slowed further still, legs and heart growing weary, oxygen sucked from the air as though the house sat atop a hellish, forbidding mountain. Howard forged ahead and, looking past him, the glint of glass became the glint of watching eyes and the dawn chorus whispered a warning too low to be heard. By the time he reached the waiting figure at the top of the stairs, the house had turned grey again and behind every dark pane of glass, a watcher watched with infinite patience.

The man was almost, but not quite, old. He stood stiff and formal, dressed in black suit, white shirt and plain dark tie. His hands were clasped to his front and he bowed his head to the Inspector. 'Sir Charles is ready for you, Inspector. Please follow me.'

The man ignored the boy as though he didn't exist. If this was truly his home, then why was he ignored so? As he approached the house Tom's mood continued to darken. He tried and failed to find that elusive connection with the place that had to be there. This was his home after all.

They crossed a cavernous tiled hall and then the policeman's clacking shoes were muffled by the thick carpet of a large but simply furnished room on the other side. An unlit fireplace, sterile white walls and a large gilded mirror over the mantelpiece defined the space. Evenly spread in a neat line around the walls, dozens of framed photographs showed a man shaking important hands and smiling important smiles. One of those smiles belonged to the policeman who had brought him here.

The butler, Jason the Inspector had called him, gestured to a small burgundy sofa and ushered Tom to sit. In the same movement he nodded to Howard. 'If you follow me Inspector, Sir Charles will see you immediately.'

The policeman glanced at Tom and smiled reassuringly. 'Will you be OK?' he asked.

Tom nodded. He was still numb and welcomed the time alone. The two men left and Jason closed the door behind him. Suddenly remembering the last time someone did that, Tom crossed the room and tried the handle. It was open. Breathing easier he turned and studied his surroundings.

Bright as the room was, Tom was struck by the silence, enhanced it seemed by the tick, tick of a large grandfather clock swinging its pendulum in the corner to the right of a huge bay window.

He thought of Katriana, wondering how he could see her, when he remembered the photograph of his sister. Howard had told him nothing and probed him at length about the girl. It seemed, on reflection, more of an interrogation than a gentle condescending debrief. The policeman did not appear to believe that the boy remembered nothing and to be fair, Tom had not exactly told the complete truth.

Looking out the massive window, he thought hard about what it all meant.

The pictures used in the search were old. Was he really to believe that he and his sister had somehow lived all this time without ageing? Something deep and profound inside told him that the idea was not as fanciful as it first seemed.

He scanned the view outside, hoping to see something that would hook a memory.

The window faced the front lawn where the helicopter had landed. There, standing at the top of the curved steps where the butler had greeted him, an old man shuffled painfully at the policeman's side. He was bent, an ebony cane topped with ivory held in his right hand while his other elbow was supported respectfully by Howard. Like this, they descended the steps with slow care, all the time talking; their heads close in conspiratorial communication. They disappeared from view for a few moments and reappeared beyond the rise on the other side of the driveway. There, huddled close like old friends, they sat on a bench looking onto the lawn and the forest beyond.

Tom wondered what they were talking about. He supposed the policeman was updating the old man about Tess. As he thought about this, Tom suddenly realised that he did not know what the relationship between him and the old man actually was. As he pondered this puzzle, a white police car drew gently along the drive towards the house. The pair on the bench stood, the old man gripping the younger's hand in both of his. Howard opened the passenger door and ducked inside. The car drove on, completing a circle round the lawn before it was re-swallowed by the forest; disappeared as though it was never there.

At the sight of the empty drive, Tom suddenly felt wary. A nagging unease had been building and now he felt alone and defenceless.

He had been staring at the spot where the road entered the forest and had not noticed the old man's painful ascent of the stone steps. But suddenly there he was, no more than fifteen metres from the window where he stood. The stranger looked his way and their eyes met. The wrinkled mouth turned upwards, the watery gaze steady and warm. The old man was pleased to see him.

His posture seemed to improve then and the shuffling and painfully slow gait became more of a tired limp and George Silas entered the house to meet the boy he had lost so very, very long ago.

THIRTY THREE

There was something about the old man that unsettled Tom. He looked ordinary enough with wispy white hair and skin as tough and crumpled as tree bark. There was indeed an intangible quality that was familiar to him, a something that made the boy queasy when his host entered the room and sat in an armchair by the barren hearth.

He did not offer his hand but smiled benignly at Tom as he gestured to the sofa opposite him with the tip of his quivering cane. 'Sit.'

Tom took the seat, backed as far as he could to the far end, trying to distance himself from the growing sense that something was wrong. The vague connection he felt was not one of warmth and love but of loss and he was the loser.

'I'm told this is my home,' he said, his voice breaking for what seemed to be no reason at all.

'Do you not recognise me, boy?'

The word *boy* seemed to crawl from the old man's mouth in letters of putrid smoke. Tom shook his head and the illusion vanished as quickly as it had appeared. The horror it dredged from Tom's fractured emotions remained strong and he found himself scanning the room for a means of escape from a threat he could not put his finger on.

'I.. I can't remember.'

'No, you wouldn't.'

The old man smiled. 'I've changed a little since we last saw each -
'

'No,' Tom interrupted. 'I mean I don't remember anything. Or at least not much.'

'I know what you mean, boy!' There was a sudden venom in the old man's voice and it brought back the sickness he'd felt earlier. His stomach heaved in reaction to a subliminal fear.

'Who are you?' Whatever was happening, Tom was suddenly tired of being led around as though he had no stake in his own future. First Chief Inspector Howard and now this nasty old man.

The tick, tick, tick of the old clock amplified the silence and Tom stared into the cruel eyes opposite, determined to fight the impulse to look away. And somewhere, recognition came and went in an instant of connected memories that failed to make it to the surface.

The old man ignored Tom's question.

'You must be tired and hungry.' He wrinkled his nose. 'And you smell as though you haven't bathed in a thousand years.'

He seemed amused by something and then rose on shaking legs, pushing down with both hands on the ivory carving of the cane.

'You haven't answered me,' Tom said, all sense of pretence, of inappropriate sensibilities, gone. The old man passed him by.

'We have much work to do and you are useless to me in this state.'

But if he didn't quite know who he was dealing with yet, Tom felt the full force of his hatred bubble from a festering wound he could not ignore.

He reached out and grasped the man's hand as he passed his place on the sofa. He had only intended to stop him leaving, to get him to answer his question, but on touching the flesh, the contact was all he needed to know the horrific truth of who he was.

As skin touched skin, Tom saw himself sitting in a high-backed chair, felt his wet feet, the cradle at his neck and Tess' comforting grip on his other side. He gasped, withdrew his hand and jumped to his feet.

'You!'

Tom backed away and found himself pressed up against the old clock, its tick and tock unaffected by the dramatic events it marked with relentless precision.

In almost every way possible the man standing before him looked nothing like the one he'd seen in his imagination but he knew now, without a doubt, that the old man was George Silas. He was ancient and weak and to Tom, it seemed, physically powerless. He could smash him aside with a simple sweep of his hand. But some deep flaw froze him to inaction and threatened to vacate his bowels.

The primitive urges to fight or flee tussled and held him back until Silas stood in front of him, his face pressed towards his, the benign smile now ugly and triumphant, lines of saliva hanging like spidery thread between upper and lower lips. 'I've been waiting for you, Tom. We need each other, you and me. Now tell me – '

But Tom had recovered enough to move. He ducked under the old man's arm and ran for the exit.

'Stop!' Silas yelled but Tom's hand was already twisting the handle, pulling the door. Out of the corner of his eye, he saw a movement that brought back the terrible memory of Kathleen and Tess' ordeal by the cave entrance. Silas raised the cane and pointed its tip towards the boy but at such a distance, Tom felt safe and threw himself from the room. As he did, a short shooshing sound came from the old man's position and a mild sting like a mosquito bite slapped the back of his hand as it slid around the edge of the wood. The sting turned to fire that spread throughout the boy's body. He jerked spasmodically, flailing on the carpeted floor, his muscles contracting and relaxing to the random crackle of electric shocks. He lay helpless, half aware of the shuffling gait of the old man walking towards him. Through twitching and uncontrolled vision, Tom saw the glint in Silas' eye, the joy of the prodigal return. He was happy - very happy.

'My boy,' he croaked. 'My boy. Home at last.'

THIRTY FOUR

Tom lay on a small bed. There were no sheets or blankets but an unzipped sleeping bag half covered his still-dressed body.

The space was small and bare; a cell more than a bedroom. He rolled up and swung his legs over the side. His muscles ached and when he stood, the room pitched as he swayed in giddy circles with his feet pinned to the floor. He reached out and placed a hand against a wall, supporting himself for a count of ten before trying to stand upright again.

Still dizzy, but recovering fast, Tom found a door and tried it. This one was locked. He heard noises from the other side. Someone was moving about. He was wondering what he should do - to call out or lie down and think - when the old man's caustic voice sounded through the wood. 'Good. You're up.'

Tom stepped back. The door swung open and Silas stood with a glass of milk in one hand and his cane in the other.

'Did you sleep?' he asked - a concerned, chain-smoking grandfather on a bright suburban morning.

Tom looked beyond him. He was on the edge of what looked like a lab. There were benches and computers, machines with shiny tubes and flashing lights. And there was a cubicle, a transparent door enclosing a seat that instantly brought the loathing he felt for the vile creature in front of him to an explosive and violent outburst beyond his control. He knocked the glass from the old man's hand and ducked right, preparing to strike his gaoler with a left fist before he could bring his cane up. But although Tom moved fast and the old man hardly twitched from his position by the open door, Tom's knees suddenly buckled and he collapsed, convulsing and in pain where he had stood.

'You can fight me all you want, boy. If we have to start from the beginning, then so be it, but I know, and soon you will too, that the lessons are still there.' The pain vanished and Tom stopped wiping the spilled milk with his flailing body.

'We'll try again.'

He nodded to the cell. 'Shower and change. You will then eat. Do not make me hurt you again - I need you well. We'll continue when you are refreshed.'

Continue what?

Silas closed the door, Tom scrambling back from his spread-eagled spot half-in and half-out of the doorway.

That was *lesson one*, thought Tom.

As he hauled himself to his feet, Tess' nagging look came streaming back to him and finally hit its mark. There was so much he did not understand but he knew for certain that whatever George Silas wanted from him, Tom would never win by blundering blindly through fear and anger. He had to control himself. Be strong. Clever.

Lifting himself up, he found the shower, innocently camouflaged in the far corner of the room by a sliding door coloured the same light-blue as the walls.

He stripped his milk-sodden clothes and embraced the needle-hot-water of the shower. The jet was high pressure, a hundred points pricking his skin, a hundred micro-massagers sweeping away the negative tension that had been with him for days. He seemed to have known little else in his short and troubled life. As he soaped his aching body, Tom felt a slight bump under his left armpit. He examined the spot as best he could amid the steam. Whatever it was, Tom knew it was not a natural part of him and was just as certain that it had not been there before. He recalled the pain he'd suffered minutes earlier and now convinced himself that it had started under that arm.

Towelling his body and drying the spot carefully, he located a tiny puncture that looked as innocuous as a freckle. Silas had injected something into him. The skin was tender to the touch, still aching from the crippling shock Silas had forced through his body. The realisation that he was completely at the man's mercy threatened Tom's resolve. What now his hope of escape? What now his futile anger when he thought of Kathleen and Tess?

Then there was that look again. Tess. The strength of one girl matching and boosting his. And he felt shame at his own weakness.

He stilled the panic threatening to cripple him as surely as the thing inside him. He would think and plan and then he would act. There was nothing he could do about the implant now, but he recognised that knowing was better than not knowing. It was a start.

He found a shirt and jeans; both a little loose, but clean and fresh. The only thing Silas had left out was new shoes but apart from being a little stained on the outside, his boots were comfortable and Tom felt, physically at least, much stronger than he had when he'd awoken. His mind was also clearer. He was learning - really learning. Difficult as it was, Tom had to fight the reflex notion that anything the hateful creature said to him should be rejected without thought. The man had been right about his need for rest. He felt rejuvenated by the shower and clean clothing and now he also felt ravenous. When Silas brought him another glass of milk, Tom thanked him and let the cool liquid wash his throat and fill his stomach in one ecstatic long tilt.

Silas smiled, savouring another little victory. 'Are you hungry?'

Tom nodded.

Silas shuffled aside and as Tom walked past him, he noticed the man fingering a ring with nervous twitches that did not reveal itself on his face. That small observation told him two things. One - Silas was not as confident as he seemed to be and two - the ring was more than just an ornament. Suppressing the thought from appearing on his face, Tom wondered if the ring held the key to his sudden pain. His mind began to race and to plot and plan as he walked quietly into a small lounge to do as he was told and eat the meal his master had provided for him.

And the meal was delicious.

THIRTY FIVE

'I won't hurt you.'

Tom's eyes widened as Silas brought the needle closer. The morning had passed in a blur and although he knew that the truce between the pair was an illusion as thin as the trust they had in each other, each hour in this state brought him closer to learning what he needed to know and gave him his best shot at getting away from the maniac he refused to call *Father.* If Kathleen was not his real mother, he could not be born of the same blood as Silas. No way.

Curiously, after questioning Tom on what he knew of Tess' whereabouts, Silas had left the subject alone. This, despite Tom's efforts to find out all he could about his absent and mysterious sister. There were, according to the man, more pressing matters to be dealt with.

And now, apparently, the most pressing of them all was to stick a needle the size of a sausage skewer into his arm and draw his blood. Tom wanted to run but knew it would be useless. He would be brought down by the thing buried in his flesh and the blood would be taken anyway. He took a deep breath and tried to use the event to his advantage. Confidence and trust was the key. He had to fake both.

As the needle penetrated his vein, Tom watched the blood fill the clear tube. He tried to ignore the revulsion he felt for Silas's touch and spoke softly as though to his doctor. 'Is there something wrong with me?'

Silas chuckled. 'I hope not.' He kept his eye on the red flood in the tube. 'You, boy, are my salvation.' Tom caught a strong smell of raw onions and gagged back a choking cough.

'I thought I was going to go mad,' continued Tom.

He wanted to know what the man was doing but had learned that the best way to get him to talk was to give him a nudge and then step back. He was also keen to find out more about Kathleen and Creggan. Who he was.

'I'm afflicted by time.' The syringe full, Silas withdrew the needle from the boy's arm and straightened himself to a hunch. He brought the liquid close to his eyes and smiled. 'Age is the greatest disease there is.' He looked at Tom, the smile broadening to an expectant grin. 'And you, boy, are the cure for many things.'

He took the blood and carefully injected it into a machine the size of a small car. Gleaming and polished pipes curved sensuously from one part to another. A monitor and keyboard formed the control panel and a membrane like a cap made from a thick rubber balloon covered the entrance to a small box labelled *SAMPLE*. The needle pierced the cap and Silas emptied the plunger with a slow continuous push.

Tom watched in fascination. He had thought about how old he was ever since he'd uncovered the emotions linking him to Creggan's past and wondered if that is where he truly belonged.

Was Silas telling him it was true? Had he really lived all that time and not aged?

He remembered then, his injuries under the cliff and how, according to Katriana, he had arrived at the cottage without a scratch.

'How old am I?' Tom said at last.

Silas was distracted. He sat at the monitor and typed commands onto the keyboard. A low humming noise filled the air and coloured graph-like bars appeared on the screen. As the seconds ticked by, the relationship between the bars grew and shrunk until the one on the far right labelled *Telomere 97x* and coloured bright yellow, dominated the screen.

He pressed another key and a similar graph, the largest bar representing something called *Nanophage 205*, filled the space. A third screen highlighted stem cell levels. Tom tried again. 'I know I used to live above Creggan with Kathleen and Tess and... and you. How old am I?'

Silas looked up from the screen, slightly annoyed by the intrusion. 'I ask the questions. You answer.'

'But I want to learn,' Tom said, remembering the phrase Silas himself seemed so fond of.

The man stood and moved to the right side of the machine and watched with satisfaction as a dark liquid dripped into a clear tube jutting from a box labelled, *Serum.* As it filled with the speed of glacial creep, Silas seemed to ponder Tom's question and eventually, plugging the drip, drip of bloody time, he said: 'It's not that simple. Depends how you measure it. But I would say fifteen.'

The answer shocked Tom in its banality

'But,' Tom began and then didn't know quite what to say. *But what?* He changed tack. 'How old are you?'

'A lot older than I look.'

Tom was tempted to say two hundred years then but he held himself back. He almost choked when Silas followed his statement with what sounded much like Tom's sarcastic thoughts. 'A good guess would be around two hundred years.

Tom tried to take this in. *Silas was two hundred years old. Tom was fifteen.*

If this was true - and Tom reminded himself not to dismiss what the man said out of hand - that put Silas firmly within the time-scale proffered by Kathleen's journal, the cave and the ruin above Creggan. 'Is my.. I mean Kathleen. Is she alive?'

Silas tilted his head back and laughed. 'You can be quite stupid, boy. How...?' And he stopped talking, his face twisting in studied thought. 'You remember?'

Tom was about to tell him about finding the journal and then realised that Silas would know that he had also been in the cavern. He checked himself and said instead. 'A little. The ruin above Creggan Cottage. It reminded me of... things.'

This seemed to satisfy the old man and he took the cylinder marked *Serum* and placed it on a stand by the monitor. Tom was trying hard to think ahead, to look around innocently, to keep the man talking so that he could learn everything he could. Come what may, he would escape. Perhaps that is why he did not notice the knife in Silas' hand. When the wrinkled fingers wrapped Tom's right arm, the boy was more concerned with the revulsion it invoked than the thought of protecting himself. The nails dug into his wrist and Silas twisted Tom's arm outwards in a surprisingly swift motion.

And then he saw it. One minute the other arm was at Silas' side and the next it streaked up, fluorescent light glinting from its razor-sharp blade. In two smooth strokes, the weapon sliced deep into Tom's arm; his brain desperately trying to process what had just happened.

There was no pain. Not at first. The cuts were surgically clean, slicing skin and muscle, vein and tendon. His middle and pointing fingers dropped open and Tom looked at Silas with a mixture of hate and fear for what would come next.

THIRTY SIX

'Do you want me to help you or not?'

Tom lay on the floor, a trail of blood pooling around him. Silas seemed annoyed and contrite at the same time. 'I should have warned you but you can be such a baby.'

Tom shook uncontrollably and gawked at the twin lines of flesh parting like tiny red seas across his forearm.

Silas had the serum in his hand now, the blade laid theatrically on a bench and beyond the man's immediate reach.

'Look at the blood, boy. Look at it!' Unable to take his eyes from it, Tom wondered what he could mean. He thought he was going to die from massive bleeding but as he tried to focus on what Silas was getting at, he suddenly realised that the spurting liquid was turning from bright red to a treacly-black before his eyes. The bleeding stopped seconds later and became a weeping, scabbing wound with black streaks gelling like stalactites between his underarm and the floor.

'See. I wouldn't hurt you, boy. We need each other.'

He approached Tom slowly, all the while trying to reassure him that he was going to be all right. Tom stared at his mutilated arm and then at the serum coming ever closer.

At last, trembling like a drying dog, his arm met the phial and a small drop of dark liquid spilled into the single cut above his wrist.

Silas stood back, a smile of satisfaction playing his lips.

Tom stared at the gashes and as he did, the liquid seeped into the skin and a green goo flooded the canyon to cover the complete site. Second by second, with the speed of a moving watch-minute, the green turned to yellow and to blue and then pink. It hardened in some places and softened in others. And then the homogeneous area turned to a thousand autonomous blobs bubbling, multiplying, splitting and joining at their own pace, knitting and sewing his body like tiny pulsating boils on the flesh of a devil. Tom held his arm out straight, supported by his left hand. He was horrified and fascinated by the process and almost puked as the boils burst in coordinated waves and a multicoloured mix of pussy bio-fluid again swamped the area and the process ran its course once more.

'Wonderful. Perfect,' Silas rasped. He stood round-shouldered and clapped his hands repeatedly around the phial in childlike excitement.

The world seemed to pause as wave after wave of the macabre process started and progressed to the stage of pussy bursting boils until finally, some time that seemed only minutes later, the final scab fell away to leave a patch of skin, in perfect health. No scar, no wound. Nothing. Just like his cut shoulder, his bruised ankle.

Only then did Tom switch his attention to the other cut. In the few minutes it took to heal the first wound, the second, untreated cut, had formed a deep and semi-crusted black gash that had begun the same healing process but slowed to the pace of budding fruit.

And the pain! It was not specific to his arm but swept throughout his body in sickening waves. He felt as though his whole system was being raped of its resources, plundered and left weak to defend and rebuild his arm. He shivered - fear and fever squabbling for control. And as he fought back the bile and vomit threatening to erupt from his stomach, his head suddenly swayed, the lab rolled sideways and Tom's world slipped away in sweet, sweet deliverance.

*

According to Silas, Tom was out for no more than an hour. He lay where he had been left. Considering Silas' determination that he should be rested and well, his treatment of the boy was callous. This did not surprise Tom. Blood crusted the floor around him and matted his clothes.

He could not see Silas at first but heard him whistling tunelessly behind the large machine he had used to create the serum. He looked at his arm and was dismayed to see that the second wound, although remarkably improved, was still damaged. He could now move his forefinger but the middle still held tight and useless in the centre of his bloody hand.

He tried to stand, cradling his arm, succeeding only when he rolled onto his knees and wiggled up with his back to the wall.

Silas looked over to him from his position at the monitor but said nothing and went back to work.

The boy's arm throbbed. He approached the man cautiously, his eyes on the bloody knife lying to the side, now within reach of a sudden stretch.

'You're a mess,' the man said without looking up.

'I need some more serum,' said Tom, 'I.. It hurts like hell.'

'It hurts nothing like hell, boy. Clean yourself up.'

'But the serum. It worked so well. Please, it'll stop the pain.'

'There's none left.'

Tom looked at the man, confused and only then noticed something different about him. He seemed to sit straighter, his voice no longer swimming in wet phlegm.

He spied the phial then, lying close to the knife that up 'till now had held every second of his attention. It was empty. He swung an accusatory stare at the old man and the old man stood, his hunch gone, sweat slicking his face, beads of glass lining his top lip and his forehead and running misplaced tears down his cheeks. His shirt was stained, sticking to his scrawny body and he glowered at Tom daring him to challenge his authority.

'I said clean yourself up. You're pathetic.'

Tom eyed the knife and through clenched and chattering teeth, Silas smiled a mirthless smile and fingered his ring. Tom cradled his arm, turned on his heel and retreated to the little room.

THIRTY SEVEN

There were no more clothes to change into but Tom soon realised he could pick most of the blood free of the cloth by peeling it like a dried scab from skin. His arm throbbed, his heart thrummed and his head searched for an idea. Anything. He splashed his face and used his old clothes to wipe up the milk at the door. He thought about the knife, lying unattended in the lab. And he thought too, about what had just happened.

Silas had used Tom and Tom suffered for it in more ways than one. But distanced from the events, he was excited too. He was not crazy after all. He had been injured on his journey to Creggan and something in his blood had the power to heal his wounds, fast. The machine next door concentrated the effect and Silas had tested it on him before taking the serum himself. The man's cynical reassurance to Tom that they needed each other slapped him in the face. He didn't need Silas but Silas sure as hell needed him. This realisation liberated Tom. It freed his anger and gave it focus. He was the powerful one. He would not lie down defeated.

He burst from the room and approached Silas as he sat at the monitor.

'I need this,' he announced picking up the syringe.

Silas grabbed his ring-finger but Tom stood firm. 'I'm in pain. I can't help if I can't think for the pain.'

He plunged the needle into the crook of his arm, tapping the vein first time as though the action was routine. He got lucky. Blood flooded the tube and Silas loosened his grip on the ring.

Pulling the syringe free, Tom inserted it into the machine, copying Silas' procedure as near as he could recall. Turning to the monitor, Tom noted a flicker of satisfaction live and die on Silas' lips. The boy had no idea what to do next.

'I told you we needed each other,' the man said, typing as he spoke.

Tom held back his bile and said 'Thanks.'

Fifteen minutes later, Tom spread a small droplet of serum onto his wound and ten minutes after that, he was perfectly whole, his skin smooth, his fingers, his wrist, his arm fully mobile and in control. Silas however, was too preoccupied with his own health to notice Tom's recovery. Amazing as it was, it was not as amazing as Silas' own.

The man was ill, his ancient skin blackened, crumbling by the minute. Stomach cramps doubled his creaking frame over the keyboard. If it had not been for the ever-threatening ring gripped, as it was, at Silas' stomach, Tom would have run from the lab as though it was about to blow.

Instead, he slipped the serum into his pocket and coveted the knife with envious eyes.

Silas saw the look and grinned through his pain.

'Try it, boy. Try it.'

Tom backed away and sat down in a chair close by.

'Can I help?'

'Soon.'

So much menace in one little word. As Tom wondered what lay ahead, Silas doubled over again, his face stretched in pain. Without thinking, Tom stepped forward to help him but Silas jumped to his feet, faced the boy, spitting orders and twisting the ring like a worry bead. Tom flinched, expecting the pain to follow.

'Inside,' Silas yelled. The man's knees buckled and he staggered forward, recovering just enough to push Tom towards the small cell once more. Could Tom rush him, pull his hands apart before he could activate the thing? It was a one-shot chance. If he failed it would be over. Any pretence of trust, any hope of lulling the man into relaxing his guard would be gone. Somehow, Tom knew that the enraged boy of his dreams would have taken the chance without thought. But the new Tom had a plan. Fighting the triumphant fantasy of the boy-victor standing over the vanquished and dying creature at his feet, he allowed himself to be pushed across the lab. One thing at a time, he told himself. Stay calm.

He returned to the cell, and Silas, shivering, staggering and doubled-up with cramps, slammed the door and turned the key.

Tom slid his back down the door and breathed deeply, not quite believing that he'd got away with what he had just done.

He removed the serum from his pocket, studied its contents and smiled as Silas thrashed outside, moaning in agony and generally acting like a big, big baby.

*

It took Tom a few minutes to find something that would do the trick. He found it in the plastic bottle of the shower gel. Emptying its contents in the sink, Tom cleaned it and placed it on the floor. The plastic was hard, the product surprisingly cheap for such a grand house. It cracked in multiple directions and crumpled to a crazy-paved mess in one stamp of his foot.

Tom retrieved the mangled debris and ripped a likely piece in his hands.

It was sharp, with multiple forks giving the impression of broken glass. It was stiff though and large enough for the purpose he had in mind. He would have to be careful not to break the thing while it was in use. Placing the phial on the floor within reach but out of accident range, he slid the bathroom door closed and set his plan in motion.

It was one thing to imagine the pain and difficulty of the operation but quite another to live through it and make it happen.

He hyperventilated for a count of ten - in, out, in out - in short panting bursts, building his courage, delaying the pain.

And then he did it.

THIRTY EIGHT

His first attempt was a mess. Forced to use his left hand and too timid to grip the makeshift instrument tightly, the plastic sawed his palm as it slid its ragged edges over his skin.

Dropping the stinging sliver, Tom calmed himself and tried again. He placed two quivering fingers under his armpit and located the device. Concealed under a thin layer of flesh, it felt like a loose piece of bone, lightly tethered to its surroundings, floating under his touch in a small circle of freedom.

Recovering the cutter, Tom repositioned it in his hand and tightened his grip until his knuckles stood proud and white and a small trickle of blood dripped from its protruding tip and onto his stomach. He brought it to his side and pushed the congealing fluid and then the sharp underlying point of plastic against his flesh. Hands shaking, he felt the skin puncture. It was one thing to pierce himself in anger with a fine needle, quite another to butcher his torso with a scraggy dagger. The sensation of the sudden puncture caused him to jump and just as suddenly the plastic blade slipped sideways and snapped in two.

Tom almost screamed in fright. To him, the noise was that of a rifle-shot. He had hit a bone or perhaps the device itself and now, as well as a ripped and weeping wound, he was cursed with a shard of shampoo shrapnel jutting from his body underneath his arm.

Thankfully, on stealing himself to look carefully at the damage, he was able to tease the debris free with ease.

Taking no time to reflect, terrified more by the thought of failure than what he was doing, Tom grabbed another piece of the bottle and tried again. The scalpel of choice this time was a side length running from the top edge of the container to the bottom corner to form a thin pointed scoop that could have been designed to cut tiny samples from Arctic Ice. Ignoring the blood, the pulsating pain and the slippery shard digging into his fumbling right hand, he studied his work as he dug the scoop inwards at a shallow angle. He tried to gouge the device from his flesh as though it was a winkle, but it was no use. There was no way this would work. All he succeeded in doing was to push the thing deeper into his body and rip his skin to slimy shreds.

Finally, shaking the fog of fading consciousness from his mind and the tears obscuring his vision, he found another, sharp-edged shard, eased it under his skin and pulled it up and outwards with a powerful and careless stroke as though he was cutting open a football with the wrong side of a blunt knife. His skin ripped, blood flooding his side and dripping to the floor. The liquid congealed to black gunge.

Tom needed to rest, to lie back and recover from the brutality of his actions, but he could not afford the time. Trembling, he pulled the skin apart with his fingers, rolling a flap of white gristle out of the way as he searched for the pain maker. And then he had it. Slicked in sticky fluid and attached to his body with green fleshy blobs, he manoeuvred a piece of plastic between it and one of his ribs and yanked hard and fast. One end detached immediately and, two attempts later, he rolled the thing in his fingers and smiled a smile of triumph and satisfaction. This was the route to his salvation. He was going to enjoy watching Silas' face when he realised that the 'boy', as he liked to call him, was no longer in his control.

With his moment of congratulation over, Tom lay full length on the floor, damaged side up. He dabbed a tiny drop of serum onto the wound, laid his head on the floor and closed his eyes.

Somehow - he couldn't think how it was possible through the discomfort and stress - he closed his eyes and slept.

*

Something beyond the cell awoke him. It took Tom a number of seconds to remember where he was. He looked under his arm, only slightly amazed but enormously gratified to see no sign of a wound. Scattered around him, scabby pieces of broken plastic matched the black mess covering his skin and floor. He jumped to his feet, frightened that Silas would discover what he had done. Splashing himself quickly at the sink, he cleaned the dried blood and tidied the bathroom.

Finished, he dressed and returned to his bed and lay looking at the ceiling, thinking ahead to his next move. Dreaming of the shock he would give the decrepit bully masquerading as a father. He wondered when he should do it. The man was getting stronger. He saw that, even through the sickness and cramps raging through his body. He remembered how weak he had felt when his own defences had been marshalled to fix his arm, how awful he felt now. What must Silas be like? His whole body assailed by a call to arms. His antibodies ordered into action, not on one spot or another but on his varicose veins, his decaying brain, his jaundiced skin, worm-holed bones, rotten teeth, diseased eyes, his shrivelled frame and poisoned plasma - an ancient catalogue of damage accrued over two centuries. But Tom had little doubt that the weakness would be temporary. He had to make his move before the man recovered.

And then there was the iconic chair, the symbol of his family's suffering.

He could not bear the thought of spending one second sitting in that chair. He would act before then. He had to.

This thought was brewing when the lock turned and the door crashed open, slamming hard against the inside wall of his cell. Tom jumped to his feet in fright, worried that guilt was written in his eyes. He focused on his anger and set to tame it. Better repressed aggression than betraying himself by shying away from what he was about to face.

He saw a foot first. There was nothing special about the foot. It belonged to George Silas. The same sober brown shoe covered the same foot but even before the rest of him followed that step into the room, Tom knew that the man was very different to the creature he had left curled on the floor. The movement was crisp, sure and swift.

George Silas strode forward and turned to look at Tom.

He smiled and spread his arms as though to embrace the boy. But the two stood still, Tom in shock at the recovery he had hoped would take an age. A middle-aged man, lithe and wiry, a curiously bald head, white scalp atop a baby-white face. A pale moon shining happily over expensive, old-man clothes.

Despite his resolve, despite his simmering rage, Tom shrunk inwardly as the man spoke.

'I owe you, Tom. See what great things we can do. You and me.

Together!'

THIRTY NINE

To Tom, it seemed as though he had been in Silas's grip for months and was amazed to realise that it was no more than six hours. He stood transfixed as the man, his arms still outstretched, spun on the spot and whooped joyously.

Drunk with youthful vigour, he seemed to promote Tom from prisoner to best-buddy. He suddenly announced that he would show Tom around his new home.

'You mean, I've never been here before?'

Silas moved like a hyperactive humming bird, his actions lending a skittish air to the formerly dour character underneath the still-dour clothes. He ignored Tom's question and began the tour.

The lab, Tom discovered, was constructed underneath the house in what had been a complex of cellars.

'You were always my favourite,' he told Tom as he showed him his new home. At one point, as they cruised through the deserted kitchens and exited the house onto a large patio, Silas draped his arm over Tom's shoulders and drew him close. Tom suppressed a shiver.

'You don't yet know how special you are, boy. How dear you are to me.'

'What about Tess?'

A circular wrought-iron table waited in the centre of a concrete space that looked as if it had been built for twenty. A single chair faced an expanse much like the front lawn, but without the steep embankment, the curving steps or the driveway bordering its perimeter.

'Sit,' the man ordered. Tom did as he was told, pleased to duck away from that arm. 'Wait.'

Silas disappeared into the house and emerged seconds later with a kitchen chair swinging in the grip of one hand. Practicing his new-found strength and agility, he twirled the thing carelessly and fumbled it at the last moment, the clatter of wood on flag-stone rattling the tranquil setting.

Tom thought he saw the man blush. He wanted him to relax. He wanted him to talk and so he covered the awkward silence as Silas righted the chair and sat.

'The policeman,' he said. 'Chief Inspector Howard. He told me I have a sister.'

Tom tried to remember what he'd told Silas already. If he could, he wanted to convince him that he knew almost nothing apart from a few vague memories gleaned from his time at Creggan.

Silas eyed him carefully. If he suspected otherwise, he did not show it. 'We were happy. It was a happy time. Kathleen wasn't your mother but she wished she was.'

The man stood up, circled his seat and sat down again. He then went still and looked across the lawn, his sharp focus fading to a distant stare. The young, old-man, conjured fond memories that Tom suspected clashed with reality. It was strange given Tom's fractured recollection of the hate in the man's heart and the pitiless torture he had put them all through.

The distraction gave Tom a chance to glimpse his surroundings - scan the area for that single opportunity for escape that had to be near.

He was struck by how empty, yet tidy the place was. It was too big for ten people to live in, never mind one, and there had to be a large staff to keep it so clinically barren. The lawn was immaculate, the gaps between the flagstones free of weeds, the windows clean and the kitchen spotless and tidied bare. He'd only met the butler and even he was gone. Tom assumed they had all been dismissed in his honour.

'I.. sort of remember,' he forced a smile. 'They were happy times,' he lied. Impossibly, Tom forced the horrors of the cavern, the electric prod, the manacle, the chairs - the instruments of a stolen childhood - from his mind and concentrated instead on the feelings he had for the family of three that had given him so much joy.

Silas came back and focused on the boy. He was still smiling but fingered his ring absently. Tom looked at it and stopped the warm thoughts turning to laughter. *He had no idea!*

For some reason, Silas was willing to let Tom think that they were all close but even in this lie, Tom learned an important fact. His memories of Creggan were real. He may have concluded this on his own but now it was confirmed by Silas. He had been there. Tom's body was fifteen years old but he'd lived in the middle of the 19th century. He would make sense of it later if he could but right now he needed to build on the shaky lie that Silas and Tom were father and son, picking through the memories of a happy childhood. He tried his earlier question again.

'I can't remember Tess. Are they still searching for her?'

'Don't worry, boy. She's important to... us. We'll find her.'

Tom noticed that every now and then, Silas winced lightly as though some part of his body had just twisted inside him. For a second or two, around that time, the man was incapacitated. Tom knew that Silas felt safe at those times because he thought he could bring the boy down at will. As they chatted with superficial ease, Tom tried to measure these twinges to see if he could predict their onset. At times he felt he could just get up and run. If he entered the woods, he might escape, but what then? Could he get out of there again? Would he find someone to help him? Could he go to the police?

He also needed to know more. He was torn, but for now he would watch and learn and wait. He had hoped to move before the old man recovered but that option had all but disappeared before he'd thought of it.

'I want to run some tests,' Silas said, taking control of the conversation.

'On me?'

'We need to recover your memory.'

'In the chair?'

Tom said this too quickly and he tried to calm the alarm that must have sounded in his eyes.

'You remember the chair.' This was a quiet statement and Tom knew it was pointless denying it now.

'I don't know why, but it.. frightens me.'

This angered Silas and the mask of concern dropped for a brief moment.

'Not again!'

But as soon as he exploded, he calmed and smiled. 'If the girl was here she would tell you the same. Stay calm, do as you're told and we'll get along fine.'

Tom wanted to smash the man in the face and run but he cooled his temper and agreed. 'I.. think I remember that,' he said. 'What's it for?' he asked, talking about the chair with all the innocence he could muster.

Silas suddenly jumped to his feet and said with the excitement of a child:

'Better I show you. Don't you agree?'

FORTY

This was it. Minute by minute, Tom's options were running away from him. He should have escaped by now. Telling himself that he was right to be cautious did nothing to stem the despair he felt or the frustration of his failure to act while he was outside. But it was true. Unless he could take Silas down, he would be hunted and caught. After that there would be no escape. Ever.

But here he was, back in the lab, looking at the booth. The chair.

In fact there were two chairs, one hidden by a partition holding the glass-panelled door in place. The cubicle was bigger than it looked from the oblique angle he'd viewed it from earlier. Inside, the walls were lined by tiles, patterned grey pyramided dimples like egg cartons. All the better to muffle screams.

'The first rig I made was crude. It worked, but quite uncomfortable.' As he talked, Silas busied himself at the monitor, his movements short, almost bird-like in their fidgety impatience for results.

'I had to compromise. There was so little technology available. Had to be creative. Between the three of us, we discovered enough to fix much of the damage.'

Tom was listening but his eyes continually glanced down at the knife lying beside the monitor. Silas caught him doing this but just smiled and carried on talking.

'We knew that jumping so far back would be more dangerous for me than for you and your sister. And by Satan we were right. Damned near killed me.'

He paused his flittering at the keyboard and looked straight through the monitor to another time.

Tom recalled the sphere he'd seen in Silas' thoughts, saw it swoop down on the Arran coast, the impossibly damaged man with a baby under each arm, somehow surviving to build a stone house to nurture the children and his sick mind.

'I could hardly crawl,' he rasped, 'never mind look after two bairns. She was a good woman, Kathleen. A good woman.'

Tom slid his left hand towards the knife.

'I had to be tough on her but she did a good job on you and Tessa. A good job.'

Tom's fingers approached the knife, shaking like a snake's rattle.

'You know, Tom. You're lucky you found me.'

Yeah right!

'And Tessa too.'

Tom was only half listening. Silas tapped at the keyboard, jerking his head from his two-fingered stab up to the monitor and back again as though pecking with his nose as a third digit.

Tom felt the roughened plastic handle slide under his tips.

'You would have died without treatment.'

Tom paused, only half aware of what Silas had just told him, his brain not quite grasping his words.

Tom's fingers curled around the weapon. Silas pecked at the keyboard.

'And Tessa.'

The knife felt good.

'She's like you.'

He lifted the blade, felt the pleasure of its heft.

'She's probably got, say, a week left. Maybe less.'

The weapon his, Tom looked directly at his prey. What should he do? Stick the knife in his shoulder? Threaten him? He had to put him down. He could not let him come after him.

And Silas' words played at the edges of his mind. *Tess had less than a week.*

'You're the key, Tom.'

Suddenly Silas stopped typing and looked directly at the boy.

'That's why you're not going to use that.' He nodded to the knife and Tom froze, confused by Silas' calm acceptance of the situation, wondering why he wasn't going for the ring. He hesitated long enough for Silas' words to sink deeper and penetrate his thoughts.

'Why exactly would you want your sister to die, Tom?'

Tom's fear swung to anger. He was about to run free and Silas was playing with his mind. But what if it was true?

'What's wrong with her?' he asked.

'Surely you remember how I used to look?'

Tom remembered. The man in the boat. His shuffling and crippled gait, his hunched and shrivelled body, his half-eaten face, mottled skin. The pain. The fear and anger. He shivered and tightened his grip on the knife.

'I remember.'

'We took the same journey. All of us. You, me and Tess.'

This made sense to Tom.

'When it was time to go back, I couldn't leave with you. I could not stand the journey. Not again. Not so soon. You had to do it yourselves. And I'm proud of you.'

'What are you talking about?'

Tom held the knife in front of him, its lethal point inches from Silas' bald head.

'No human has ever done what we've done before. It has its price. A terrible price.'

'What have you done with Tess?'

'You're not listening, boy. I'm not your enemy.'

Tom had the upper hand now. He was not much smaller than Silas and the man spasmed as Tom fought the urge to kill him where he sat. Stone dead. But he remembered his promise to himself. He could not assume that what Silas said was wrong just because he didn't like him or the words he spoke.

'You're speaking in riddles. What's wrong with us? What journey? Is it to do with the sphere? The light.'

Silas smiled. 'Oh yes. It's to do with the light. Good. You remembered. The sphere is our transport. It shields us from harm. It should have protected you both. Why do you think you were hurt? Your memories trashed?' He paused and held Tom's gaze for a moment before continuing, his voice a soft call to arms. 'We can fix this. We can find Tessa and help her.'

The thought of Tess in trouble haunted Tom. He eased his grip on the blade but kept it pointed at Silas.

Silas looked down and fingered his ring. 'I could bring you to your knees, Tom. Ask yourself why I haven't done that.' He swivelled his chair and stared up at the boy's face.

'I need you to trust me.'

He slowly raised a hand. Tom reset his grip and prepared for a trick. He was ready. He could do it. He *wanted* to do it!

But Silas did not lunge for the knife. He took Tom's free hand in his and, despite the revulsion he felt, Tom let him.

'I'm going to show you something, Tom. I don't believe you've lost the skills I taught you. We have a bond. The three of us.'

He gripped Tom's fingers and closed his eyes and as he did, Tom saw what Silas saw and he knew without a doubt that, this time at least, the man was not lying.

He dropped the knife and sagged to his knees. 'What do I have to do?' he asked.

'The chair. It's all we've got. Trust me. It's safe.'

Tom nodded slowly, stood and walked towards the booth.

FORTY ONE

Sitting there, the constant hum of electricity in the lab was only obvious by the sudden silence when Silas closed the cubicle door.

The lack of sound pounded his ears, his blood pulsing a beat of tense anticipation on his drums. The first thing Tom noticed was that the design of this chair was more sophisticated, less like an executioner's device than its counterpart in the cavern. His arms and legs were restrained but not with the aggression of his Creggan visions. The bands wrapping his wrists and ankles were more like contact points than shackles. The conduits were subtle but, even as the door closed, a fleeting tingle coursed his limbs and tugged the hair on the back of his neck erect.

There was no uncomfortable neck brace, no sense that if he did not obey, that he would be garrotted by an ever-tightening noose.

Silas, swinging between the extremes of hyper-kinetic stuttering and slow-burn tension, sat at the monitor, turned his head and stared long and hard at Tom.

It was as though he had lost the power of animation or was somehow trying to control Tom by thought alone.

But then that's exactly what he had done.

It would be wrong to say that the image of Tess' lonely struggle had reached out from Silas and into Tom when he'd earlier touched him. Rather, it was more the other way round. As though Silas had helped Tom to tap into what was already there, in his own head - teasing it forward to the front of his mind.

And now that he knew how to reach it, he could sense her now. She was frightened. Alone. Lying in the dark. She struggled to deal with something compelling her to a task she did not relish or understand. She was a confused automaton.

Tom caught a glimpse of her surroundings but they were dark. He had no idea where she was.

The link between them was tangible and strong. He felt her pulse slide over the pounding in his ears, the rhythm of her breath step-lock his own. Silas, too, was there, but weaker. Much weaker.

At once he had guided Tom, shepherding a power that somehow allowed him to bond with his sister without knowing where she was.

He needed the boy to find her. It was a stalemate. They needed each other.

Tom clenched his fists as Silas turned to the monitor and tapped the command to go.

*

Someone or something was inside his head. A consciousness, another self perhaps, writhed beneath the surface he had come to think of as Tom. Through the doppelgänger's eyes, he saw an explosive creation of knowledge - a biggish-bang spawning a small universe. Something popped in his brain. A miniature vessel burst, a stroke, a blockage freed. Like his strange dreams, a billion facts and images, a trillion sounds and events, grew from a nucleonic point to planetary, solar, galactic and universal sizes - clustering, imploding, pulsing - a data furnace ripping through the boy's head. Uncontrolled. Unordered. This self, the other boy, struggled against the cataclysmic genesis. Tom's muscles solidified, cramping in sympathy with the boy's struggles to control his tumbling journey through the expanse as it grew from pinpoint violence to white hot turmoil and then to a billion receding suns and a vast emptiness of spinning space - a void where up was down and down meant nothing.

And then to his left or right, a brief bullet crashed through the boy's mind. It smashed to a brilliant, incandescent glimpse of another life. An instant view of a coast of blue and green, separated by a rugged rift of rocks and sand, of pebbles and clustered memories. He was home, at Creggan. Below him, Katriana was sitting on the rock watching the hill for his return. And as quickly as the image smashed through his head, another missile passed, neutrino-like, through the soles of his feet and flashed a picture of a tortured face before leaving his mind broiling in conflict at the rapid change in mood the discordant views conjured there. And then a parcel of noise, laughter and then another, a scream, and then another, a cry of pity, a feeling of joy, of anger, of agony and ecstasy. The flow of atomized smells, random views, sudden sounds and unconnected snippets of being, came and went beyond his control.

And as the onslaught continued, as each slice of life wrought havoc with his emotions, an intruder pushed his way through the barrage and gripped the boy's wrist with bony fingers. The intruder pulled him from the centre of the furnace to the quiet shore at the edge of the cauldron where Tom could suddenly breathe and for the first time since he closed his eyes, really look around at the strange world surrounding him.

What he thought had been universal objects obeying Newton's laws of motion were nothing of the sort. Sparkling clusters of light grouped together, but their movements were not planetary. This discrepancy disorientated Tom even more than he had been. His mind was slowly catching up with what he was seeing when Silas did something at his side and the confusion disappeared. The lights ordered themselves to the universe he expected and at his feet, a blue planet, bright and beautiful hung in space and filled his vision.

Silas tugged Tom's wrist and, together, they dropped like missiles towards the planet he knew was Earth.

Below them, the orb spun quickly, one way and then another, and soon the air swept his hair, cool and fresh, his cheeks flapping like a sky-diver's - an ocean and then land and then ocean again. Ships and cities. And now they slowed. An island. Forest and mountain. He recognised the grey plunging rocks of Arran and then the subtle depression below the trees and the house, its crenellated walls imposing a look of a fortress on the place.

Silas and Tom passed effortlessly through the roof, the floors, and Tom watched with fascination as they entered the lab, the man reuniting with his own body and Tom with his.

Tom opened his eyes and looked through the glass door. Silas returned the look and smiled benevolently.

He did not move his lips, but Tom heard him as clearly as if he had.

'Perfect, boy. Perfect. Now we can begin.'

FORTY TWO

Tom could sense Tess just as he had when Silas had touched him a few minutes ago and when he had begun this strange journey from cavern to lab rat.

The sense of her was the same. She was still in the dark, still confused and still operating on automatic pilot. It was different too. There was a direction to the link and he desperately wanted to follow it. Without thinking what he was doing, or how, Tom drifted upwards from his body, curiously noting the boy below him looking ahead as though nothing was more natural.

He did not think of Silas, had no inkling or interest in whether the man would follow him to his sister's location or not. What he did not expect was a restraining hand pulling him gently to Earth until he was back in the booth, back inside his body on the chair. He could have struggled, and Tom was quite sure he would have won, but the man was guiding, not bullying him and somehow, to Tom, this made all the difference. Whatever this strange power and whatever his thoughts on Silas, it was he who had brought him to this place and he who had shown him the power of Tom's own mind. It seemed perfectly natural to let him lead now. After all, they both wanted the same thing. They both wanted to find Tess.

'That's not the way, Tom.'

The words sounded in his head, but he knew they came from Silas as he tapped at the keyboard outside the cubicle.

'The journey has confused you. We need to correct that. You need to trust me until we're ready to move.'

That word *trust*, coming from Silas, jarred Tom. It was one thing to risk everything for someone he loved, something else entirely to wipe the stain of abuse from his heart.

'I can find her,' the boy said to himself and knew that Silas would hear.

'Perhaps, but if you're wrong, we'll lose time. Slow down boy and listen to me.'

Tom thought he heard Tess whimpering and with enormous willpower set his mind to listen to what Silas had to say. He would give him his chance. The situation reminded him of Katriana. She had convinced Tom to delay travelling to Lochranza when it was dark. Getting lost for the sake of a few minutes would be a disaster that might cause his sister everything. He could not live with the thought that he might have saved her, if only he had listened to Silas.

'I want you to think about your first moments here.'

Tom was confused. He was about to tell Silas this but the man seemed to know he did not understand and said. 'You told Howard you woke up below a cliff. Is that your earliest memory?'

'Before I got to Creggan. Yes.'

'We start there.'

Tom nodded. He visualised himself, waking beneath the cliff, his journey through the night, the storm, the cottage, his run over the hill and then the helicopter ride to the house. The land lay before him in his thoughts and almost immediately he found himself retracing the route, flying there as though a gliding bird until he saw himself lying beneath the steep face, unconscious, his left leg bent and tucked under his right knee, his hand covered in blood.

Tom knew that what he was looking at was a vivid and realistic memory, but the sensation was uncanny.

'Tess is not here.' He turned and looked across the water beyond the Ayrshire coast, beyond the twirling marionettes. She was out there. He was sure of it.

Silas was by his side and then drifted to the ground. He sat beside the motionless boy - the boy that was Tom's memory of himself - and he pressed rejuvenated hands to the boy's unconscious temples. As he did, and as Tom watched from a few feet above, he felt a slight pressure on his skull as though the man was actually touching him.

Tom looked back over his shoulder, the compulsion to leave this place and follow his own instincts to find his sister, almost irresistible.

He concentrated on the beat of her, noting that her breathing and his own seemed to be as one. Could she sense his presence?

And then he looked to his right, along the coast towards Creggan. Towards home. Kathleen and Tess were no longer there and Katriana and her father should be gone, too. It was pointless dreaming of what might have been, but that too had a powerful attraction for him. So close to Silas, he felt alone and deserted. The boy lying there had no idea what was about to happen to him. No knowledge of the girl destined to enter his life. He would be with her soon. In Tom's disorientation, he was jealous. Jealous of a memory. His own memory at that. Crazy at last.

Tempted as he was to look at the cottage, Tom knew that finding Tess was more important. Unable to resist the pull, he decided to act. He could wait no longer. Whatever Silas was up to, he would have to...

And then whatever choice he had evaporated with the world he looked down upon.

Tom was suddenly dragged towards his own prostrate body and merged with it. For a brief instant, he lay with his eyes closed and then the events leading up to his journey to the cliff flashed before him as though it was happening to him right now. In truth, as the journey played out before him, Tom had no idea whether he was remembering or travelling for real.

He stood atop a mountain, his sister Tess and he watching a bright ball of light glide towards them. It seemed to veer to one side and then correct itself and Tom had the sense that the girl and he were drawing it towards them. As it closed on the pair, they held their ground, unafraid.

Closer and closer it came and as it neared he saw that the ball, the size of a small car, was not an amorphous blob of light but had a strange and ever shifting texture. Its surface warped and bulged like a living bubble, its light a changing play of colours. Its surface formed and reformed; not quite an entity travelling in space but walls of light that vanished and reappeared, a constant shift of creation and extinction that drew closer and closer to the siblings willing it their way.

There was no sense of breaking through the wall. At one point the light was in front of them and the next it surrounded them. They stood in its centre, suspended from the ground, the shimmering, colours engulfing them, the mountain they stood on drifting away, dwindling in size, the surrounding land shrinking to a dot, water and mountain crushing it to insignificance. This compressed view accelerated faster and faster and soon Tom recognised the view of Earth he had shared with Silas minutes before. This time he and Tess travelled at speed away from the planet and Tom knew now that what he was witnessing - remembering - was not just an image but something that had really happened.

As he felt the journey quicken to light speed, the universe vanished and beyond the spherical wall there was nothing but black space. As quickly as this happened, the cosmos reappeared and before them, ten miles across, another sphere, this time made of a dull metal, opened and swallowed the light whole. Inside, their transport evaporated. The pair stood on a large platform watching another ball of light approach, engulf and then carry them once more beyond the strange craft hanging stationary in the middle of some indistinct point of the universe.

And so the journey continued, speeding up until everything disappeared and then another giant metal station, another transfer and another leg of the journey. On and on it went, thirteen times the sequence repeated itself and then, at last, standing on another platform, Tom and Tess entered separate spheres and minutes later, Tom opened his eyes, looked up at the cliff and wondered who and where he was.

FORTY THREE

Tom opened his eyes to a blue sky. He lay on his back and, without moving his body, scanned what he could of his surroundings.

The first thing he recognised was the man kneeling beside him. His skin was baby-white, his thin face elongated by his gaping mouth as he seemed to speak to him in slow motion. But as the words came, Tom realised that George Silas was not speaking in the conventional sense, but throwing his thoughts across the short distance between them while panting with excitement.

'The light, boy. Did you feel it?'

'I saw it.'

'But did you feel it?'

This was a strange question. Tom recounted the journey he had just recalled and could not remember what he'd actually been thinking of as the light drew towards them on the mountain.

'I saw it,' he repeated.

For a brief moment, Silas' face contorted with rage, his cheeks those of a teething child. But just as quickly, he calmed and cupped Tom's head in his hands.

'You can do this, Tom. You've done it before.'

The hands squeezed and squeezed tighter.

Tom struggled, his head tugging from side to side, trying to free himself from the unbearable pressure. Flowing from Silas's fingers, through his skull, a sensation, similar to the horror he'd experienced in the cavern, buzzed like a swarm of insects in his mind.

A wild beast - Silas - was there too, picking and swiping at the scattering points in his mind, idiotically trying to herd the data-swarm to some semblance of order as he blundered through the nest of Tom's memories.

But as Silas' frantic efforts continued, Tom suddenly found himself eavesdropping on the man in return. In opening his mind to rape the boy's thoughts, Silas was vulnerable to the same fate. But Tom was better at it than him.

With rapid and unerring accuracy, Tom found himself watching Chief Inspector Howard as he sat on the bench outside the mansion, talking to an ancient grey-haired man beside him.

A conversation that took some minutes to complete in real life was Tom's in a fraction of a second. Anger and bile rose in his stomach as the words and their meaning hit him like well-thrown rocks.

'The girl's father. He's injured. Badly.'

'So?' replied the old man.

'I need to get help in there.'

'They're dangerous,' Silas spat. 'They can wait. I need to know what the boy discovered at Creggan. I'm too close to fail now.'

'The father could die.'

'Listen *Chief Inspector*.' Silas used the title as though it was a mark of derision. 'I can unmake as easily as I made you. Prison would not suit a former policeman. We both know you're going to call off the search. You debriefed the boy alone?'

Howard nodded.

'Good. No-one knows about the girl and her father. Give me some time before you do anything. I'll take care of the boy. You just do as you're told.'

Tom sat up, a sudden fury forcing him to forget the fact that he was still, in reality, sitting in the booth in Silas' lab and not, as it seemed, under a cliff near Creggan.

He wrenched himself free of Silas' grip and punched him hard in the face.

Silas reeled back in shock, the buzzing in Tom's head suddenly gone as he broke contact. Tom pushed himself to his feet and as his hands thrust upwards from the mossy vegetation, the fingers of his right hand wrapped around a roughened stone. Without thinking, determined to kill the brute who had left Katriana and her father stranded at Creggan, he launched himself upwards. Silas staggered back but Tom did not give him time to recover. He swung the rock hard, his arm outstretched, felt the satisfying crunch of bone on stone and then the give of soft tissue as the man tumbled backwards behind a large boulder and disappeared.

Shaking in anger, awash in adrenalin, Tom spent no time pitying the monster he might have just killed. He looked at his hand, bloodied red, recognising a faint memory he had no time to focus on.

He followed Silas, determined to hurt him, determined to make sure that he was dead if he wasn't already gone.

Silas bled profusely. An enormous gash merged with a ragged depression in his bald head. The smashed shell of a giant breakfast egg.

He lay at an awkward angle, his back doubled over a spiked boulder. But he was alive. The body stirred, eyes popped wide to stare at the boy. There was no fear in those eyes, only fury. The man did not attempt to get up, not in the real sense but Tom noticed a slight blurring of his outline and he suddenly remembered that what was happening here could not be real. Even so, real or not, he knew instinctively that he'd hurt Silas, bad. The hideous creature rose, floating an inch above himself like a ghosting TV picture.

Tom was about to lose his advantage. Worse, he was certain that he could learn more from him - here and now - in this weakened state, than he ever could at any other time. It was now or never. He leapt on the man, his anger instilling a strength of mind greater than its physical equivalent in the material world. Silas' anger at last swung to shock. He jerked back to the ground, a reflex action driven by fear.

Tom grabbed the man's head. He gripped it tight either side, his palms pushing hard against the buckling skull. He felt and heard the shifting grind of gristle and bone. At the same time, Tom learned in the blink between this and Silas' sickening scream that he had lied about Tess too. He wanted Tom to take him somewhere. He wanted to know how the boy controlled the sphere.

He wanted to go home.

But as quickly as the thoughts were his, Silas disappeared. Tom looked at his empty hand, blood, smearing his fingers. He almost crumpled with the enormity of his situation.

He shook his head, knowing that he could not afford the time to sit and think. Katriana and her father needed him. And Tess, too. He had to shake himself into the present, rise from the stupor that afflicted him back in the chair.

As this realisation swung him to action, he understood that he was in great danger.

Standing on the slope looking at the white-flecked sea, a gentle breeze ruffled his hair, his body vibrated with a tense and powerful anger and his mind reeled in wild flights of comprehension and confusion. Like a fleet of Russian dolls, his worlds within worlds were so real that he had to force himself to remember he was actually sitting in Silas' lab.

He was strapped to the chair and Silas was free beyond the cubicle. He could sense the man's anger boil between them like scalding tar.

Tom did not have to journey back the way he came. He did not have to waste time retracing the route of a remembered landscape to return to the lab. Angry and determined he simply opened his eyes to see Silas leap to his feet and grasp the side of his head where Tom had hit him. There was no blood, no obvious damage, but still the man crumpled to his knees, clutching the bench for support as he went down. Tom struggled to free himself from the straps locking his wrists and ankles but even though they were not the shackles he had feared, they bound him tight just the same.

Silas pulled himself up by grasping the wooden top. His body swayed and, mid-lift, he doubled over and clutched his stomach. Tom struggled uselessly as Silas recovered, his face changing, his stature growing inch by inch. Seconds later he stood tall and turned a cruel smile on the boy. In control again, he tapped the keyboard and set Tom's world on fire.

FORTY FOUR

The pain started as nothing more than the tingle he'd felt before in his arms and legs. Four circular straps - ankles and wrists - bristled as though the fabric had sprung a weave of miniature needles stabbing his skin. Tom tensed and tried to pull away from the weirdness of the effect. It was not quite pain.

Not yet.

Rippling along his limbs, a thousand tiny hairs stood erect. Throughout his torso, his skin prickled and nauseous waves of bile squirmed in his stomach as though a living thing stirred in its pit.

As the tingle grew to an irritating itch and then to a mild burn, Tom's neck strained taut. He wrenched on either wrist, willing the bands to snap. Moments later, phantom acid washed his body and the horror began.

On the other side of the cubicle door, Silas stabbed another key with theatrical aplomb. He looked mad - a crazy conductor orchestrating a hellish band of invisible musicians, piping Tom to his grave.

Terrible as this was, the discomfort of his body was nothing to that of his mind.

The buzzing seemed to start at his fingers and toes, quickly running inwards until every inch of him was alive with subsurface points of living, crawling flesh.

His left arm, apparently stronger, pulled taut against its restraining band, the fabric thinning, crinkling, biting hard and deep, soaking red as it gouged and bled him.

Tom watched in horror as his body pimpled, boils erupting violently, his skin a seething mass of bubbling fat. Each eruption pushed outwards and each vibrated to Silas' tune, quivering wildly as though there really was an insect under every single one of them – Tom a host to the parasitic birth of ten thousand furious flies. And to his horror, blood drip-dripping on the cubicle floor, that thought became a premonition. Just above his bleeding wrist, a cluster of wiggling bumps seemed to come alive, tiny beasts thrusting outwards from his arm.

And from that small area, the cancerous spot spread, blackening and cracking, the buzzing fury amplifying the boy's rising terror. Tom pulled, snapped his hands up - both wrists bleeding now, twisting - the bands wrinkled and thin but still binding tight.

Something poked a tiny albino head through a single hole in his forearm. And then another. And another and another. Throughout his body, seen and unseen, exposed skin and hidden, they emerged. Beneath his shirt, the back of his knees and between his legs, an army of white bugs crawled from their burrows, turning their heads this way and that, brushing their antennae, unfolding, preening their wings, the noise now the sound of a million skittish violins.

And then they were free, his skin in shreds.

Each boil harboured more than one insect. Behind every birth, a hideous pale sibling followed, one trailing the other. They filled the cubicle, swarming back towards him until he was covered in the things. He clamped his mouth shut - teeth and jaws and lips locked hard, straining air through an ever-decreasing gap at his flaring nose. And they found that passage too, probing and plodding, blocking his only hope for oxygen.

This was Silas' work. What he saw, what he felt, was not real. Tom believed this. In his heart and in his head - but still they were there, still his skin bled, stripped and ripped, bubbled and burst.

This wasn't real. It was not real!

He closed his eyes, shutting the image from his sight. He tried to think beyond the cubicle, beyond Silas' tugging strings. *It was all in his head. All in his head.*

Tom saw himself leave his body, watched Silas, through blind eyes, run to the cubicle, smash his fists on the door. Tom ignored him, focused on the only thoughts with the power to lift him from that place, that state of being. And the infernal buzzing followed.

He searched his mind, an Olympian effort amidst the swarm colonising his thoughts. His mother, the glimpse fleeting, held him and twirled his well-loved self to Tess' fiddle, but now he saw the cubicle again, his skin - the white plague - Silas' mad face - all through closed eyes.

He shook his head, opened his eyelids, closed them again, buried his chin to his chest, shook himself and shook himself - but still they came. He thought of Katriana, of the door closing between them at Creggan and, as he did, Silas' rage dimmed, the heavy weight of crawling bodies lightened - the pain in his wrists a welcome sense of reality that cut through the illusion this surely was.

Katriana's dark hair, indistinct, waving gently, shiny organised smoke among the fog. He drew himself to her, strained from the seat to close the distance between them. She seemed to drift away from his face, the background of the cottage fading, her features strengthening.

Without realising he was doing it, Tom's whole body strained to follow her. He could not return to the cubicle. *Would* not return! But somewhere in his mind, the pull of the machine, Silas' hypnotic probe, threatened to rip him back. He could sense its subtle tug on his subconscious. He was about to lose it all. Katriana began to fade and somewhere inside Tom something snapped.

The buzzing stopped.

Just like that.

And in the sudden silence, in some crazy world where nothing made sense, the chair left him.

Tom had no idea what happened, the sense of it hidden amid the miasma of conflicting images, battling sounds and a deluge of sensory data making up the awful world he thought he was doomed to die in. The strange event that followed, was not in his head, but in the world that should have been solid, where time and space should have followed the rules.

Tom's eyes sprung open. He flew through the cubicle glass as though it was a projected and ephemeral barrier. But that description, almost logical in the realm of dreams, was not right. He flew nowhere. He did not seem to move at all. Rather, he sat still and the bands holding him slid back and downwards with the chair. The fabric passed through his limbs as though they, or he, were wisps of air. The cubicle leaped away from him, the lab shifted as though some giant had hauled it whole and without damage and thrust it twenty feet back and down through the earth.

The glass did not shatter, Silas remained hammering on the door and the world did not stand still for a heartbeat. In one instant, it seemed, the planet had just lurched away from him and then stopped when he hung directly over Silas' control station.

And as quickly as it happened it was over and Tom dropped like a bomb to the floor.

He twisted, thrust his arms out to protect himself and crashed into the monitor.

As he turned, he saw Silas turn too and as bright sparks slammed into his face along with toughened glass, white plastic and hard steel, Silas started to scream and Tom slipped into unconsciousness.

FORTY FIVE

Before he opened his eyes, Tom sensed that he was moving. He forced himself to remain still. Sitting on a soft seat, his head jostled gently against cold glass. The thrum of tyres on asphalt drove through his body and every few seconds he felt himself alternately lift and fall from the structure he leaned against. He ached, his battered body a patchwork of bruised blue that had somehow escaped serious injury. Every muscle was stressed and then relaxed in his effort to remain still, a feat that, although uncomfortable, allowed him to test-drive his mobility before committing himself to action.

To his right, sensing a presence he assumed was Silas, Tom remembered his dream back in the cottage. He knew then, without looking, that it was dark, headlights sweeping through canyoned trees. He tried to recall what else he had seen but a familiar voice iced his blood and he flung his eyes wide open.

'I know you're awake, boy.'

Tom lifted himself slowly from his awkward angle, the aches and pains nothing to what he had endured earlier.

'You're a fool. You've ruined everything. It could have been so easy.'

Tom looked at Silas and somewhere in his head a voice warned no one in particular:

Keep your eyes on the road.

Silas glanced sideways and made a show of fingering the ring, tap tapping it lightly against the steering wheel. Tom stared at it and realised that Silas still had no idea that it was useless. His gaze moved from the finger to the dark-eyed, pale orb glowering at him.

'What happened?' Tom managed to croak.

Looking at his tormentor, Tom almost expected to see his

mouth slide over to his cheek. This was the same hideously disfigured man that had brought so much misery to his family.

'If you'd listened to me, you'd know what happened. You would be free, your sister safe. We'd all be home.'

'I.. I don't understand.'

'You angered me. You made me hurt you.'

'I was strapped. Then I wasn't. I mean, I flew out of the chair.'

'You flew like a piece of dung, boy. You ruined everything. The terminal. Your chance of an easy ride.'

Tom felt the hackles rise at the back of his neck at these words and it was nothing to do with Silas invading his mind.

He tried to ignore the implications and probed the man for more information.

'Was it real?'

'Of course it was real!' Silas shouted this and Tom shrunk back to the door before he checked himself. He would not cower. He knew what he must do and he was going to do it.

'But the straps, the glass.'

An oncoming car swung wide around a bend and blinded them for a moment. Silas swerved but otherwise paid no attention to the vehicle as it blasted into their rear-view mirror and snaked behind them to a stop. He drove on, kicking the accelerator to the floor, swinging the wheel and the car around the bend.

'You are so close. I wanted this to be easy for you. No stress to steal your concentration.'

Tom flared in anger and frustration. He knew it was stupid but he could not help himself.

'How can I know what to do when you won't tell me!?'

Silas lifted his hand, moving automatically to the ring, but another bend forced him to re-grip the wheel and screech the curve, pushing Tom tight against the door.

'I have waited a hundred and forty years, boy. Do not try my patience. Five minutes and you would have known everything. Your temper; it makes you stupid.'

'Where are we going?'

Tom said this quietly, suddenly aware that travelling away from Silas' lab did not make sense for a man so bent on using Tom to get home.

Wherever home was.

'It'll take days to fix your mess.'

Tom was about to ask him if he had another lab somewhere when it clicked. He knew where they where headed.

'We're going to Creggan, aren't we?'

'You have a date with the girl. We wouldn't want to disappoint her.' His voice was low, the threat implicit. But still he pressed the point to Tom.

'We did it once before. I made you and your sister masters of your gift.'

An insane thrill rushed through Tom at the thought of returning to Creggan as though a part of him hoped that it would be to rescue her and not to bring a monster to her door. It disappeared almost immediately and Tom pleaded with Silas.

'No! Take me back. We'll do it together. I just... You need to teach me. Tell me what to do.' The sense of panic rose in his voice and Tom knew that he had made a mistake.

Silas grinned. 'I will, Tom,' he said. 'All we need is the right incentive and everything will flood back to you.'

They hurtled down a hill, overshadowed on either side by small grassy mountains, the one to their left close, the one on the right further back and, even in the darkness, chilling in its familiarity. Somewhere out there a path ran over the hill and down to his childhood sea.

'Katriana. That's her name isn't it? Not much younger than Kathleen when we first met.'

Tom could not let this happen. He had to get to Creggan before Silas. He'd wondered what would make him jump from a moving car and now he understood. He edged away from Silas, only partially feigning the shrinkage of his frame, fearing what the man was capable of.

In the distance, another car approached them, the second on the journey through the desolate, slumbering island.

Tom had a sudden hope that Katriana would be gone, but quickly realised that it was probably forlorn. She would have waited for him, hoping for a quick return, unable to desert her father as the hours trickled by. She could not leave the man on his own and at every moment she would have expected a helicopter, a boat, a rescue party, the police or Tom himself to appear at the cottage. Only as the day drew to a close would she decide that something had gone wrong and even then her choices were still poor. Unless her father's condition forced her to do otherwise, she would leave him to get help only when it was obvious that no-one was coming.

She would go at first light. He knew that was true as clearly as if he was standing beside her, listening to her thoughts.

His hand crept to the door handle and he pulled.

FORTY SIX

Tom heard Silas curse. The cruel voice was behind him, almost drowned by the rush of air, rubber rumbling on road. The man lurched for the ring on his hand, but in his fury and confusion fumbled the wheel before he got there. They swerved. Tom was hauled back by the unexpected inertial pull. He swung on the door. In a frozen instant, he saw Silas recover, hands now steady, finger stabbing at the ring that would bring the boy to his knees. And beyond that freeze-frame, the cruel smile spread as the bald head turned to watch his work. Tom could not help himself, the broad grin now on his face designed to infuriate his abductor. Silas stabbed and stabbed again, the smile gone, his eyes off the road, staring at the ring and then back at Tom. Once again he lost control of the wheel, his need to tether the boy the only thing in the world.

Tom leapt from the seat, diving into a burling, twirling world of sudden trees, screaming metal and snapping wood. Two feet from his head, hidden rock and spinning wheels, tyres bounced - two, four - an eerie, dreamy silence, a pre-bomb beat of dead air before Tom hit the ground. A body-crushing thud, rolling in soft, muddy grass while above him the door twisted and slammed back against the space he had just left. Headlights soared, twin cones painting the canopy. A bird caught in flight, spread wings, mid flap, a brief flash before the violent thunder of crashing, smashing metal. The cones rolled and fell. The car slewed sideways, missing the thick trunk of the tree, careering back to the curving road, crossing it, flying and flipping over a small embankment, crushing a flimsy fine-mesh fence.

As Tom tumbled to a dazed halt, he was vaguely aware of Silas' crash. He could not see, but heard the landing, a muffled crump, the crunch of glass, the high-pitched whine of an engine racing. On its roof, its back wheels spun-dry, mud splattering spray, wooden posts and steel wire either side of the car suddenly wrenched from the ground, flinging themselves at the car, pounding on its panels. The engine coughed to a halt.

Tom crawled towards the road, the world around him illuminated by flashes of brilliant white that, although in his head, gave the illusion that he was surrounded by phantom paparazzi popping their cameras to pulse the night-ground to a psychedelic, strobe-lit day. Standing slowly, he steadied his vision, oriented himself to what was around him. At first a little confused, he satisfied himself that, if he was injured, it was hidden beneath the collection of cuts and bruises he had accrued in the lab.

He stood motionless, watching the steady headlights stab the field across the road, the dim white of bobbing sheep sprinting to grey and then to black.

Tom waited for Silas to rise from the wreck. He did not consider rushing to his aid. Something within him knew that the man was alive. He had not survived all these years to die so easily. No. He was dangerous. For all Tom knew, the man was on his way to kill him, even now. He moved cautiously into the road, crossing away from the car, keeping his distance until he could be sure that the predator was not stalking towards him. Two minutes of hissing steam, cooling, ticking metal and Tom edged forward, still hugging the road, ready to hide at the first sound. But still there was nothing. Nearing the crash, Tom saw a broken branch in the wash of reflected light. He picked it up and raised it, two-handed, before him. His heart pulsing pure adrenalin, Tom felt strong. Angry. He edged towards the light.

Closer now, the doors on either side were crushed and twisted open, the roof buckled, the cabin however, as far as he could see, still large enough to hold a man.

The interior light, the flush of blue from the expensive dashboard, cast a surreal glow on the soft cream of the inverted roof.

The driver was gone.

Hackles rising, Tom spun around, expecting an attack from behind, but he was quite alone.

Everything in him told the boy to run - to get away from there as fast and as far as his feet would fly.

But he had to know.

And in some dark place, a part of him wondered what he would do with the club if he found Silas hurt and helpless. Could Tom really be the murderer he thought he was at Creggan?

Satisfied that there was no-one about to attack from the rear, Tom inched forward, ducking his head, searching for the monster that had terrorised his family, abused the title *Father*. And oh, the club felt good.

He could see the back of the seat through the open door, but still no sign of Silas. He stopped and looked around again. Listened and moved forward.

Close enough to peer through the glassless side window, Tom froze, his confidence failing with his hope of finding a wounded and helpless Silas. The cabin was empty. Confused but determined to confront the man, Tom sank to his knees, a sudden smell of fuel clawing at his throat. He peered in the back, poked his head through the gap of the tortured door. Front and rear. Silas had vanished.

Tom staggered to his feet and ran back from the light. He crouched low in the darkness, watched and listened and waited. In another time and in other circumstances he would have searched the area until he found the victim of such a crash. Perhaps he had been thrown clear, perhaps, like Tom, he'd jumped or simply left the scene dazed and confused.

But perhaps too, he was watching him now. Waiting to make his move. Perhaps he was twisting the ring, furious at the uselessness of it.

But Tom was terrified of one thing only. That Silas was already on his way to Creggan. Even if he was out there injured, would he soon recover and launch his resources - his enormous wealth and power - to get to Katriana and her father before Tom?

He would waste no more time.

Deciding what to do, he retreated back up the road, turned towards the vague outline of the mountain leading to Creggan and stumbled across the dark rough ground towards it.

FORTY SEVEN

It took Tom two hours to reach the path and in those two hours, each step carried him closer to who he was.

Skirting the accident, the boy stumbled through field and fern. The ground was mostly flat, sloping slightly from right down to left. Ahead, the grassy mountain rose unseen. There, obscured by the night, the path he was looking for cut through his direction of travel. Sooner or later, he had to cross it. Somewhere to his left, Lochranza slept and he allowed the ground to push him that way, hoping to find a small road or track leading to the path.

Countless fences crossed his route and, more than once, Tom fled from one field to another as some animal, he always assumed was a monstrous bull, lumbered towards him through the murk.

The total darkness beyond the car headlights had turned to dim shapes lurking in a world of moonless shadows. But soon, even that light vanished as a freshening breeze swept an ever thickening cloud over his head to kill the guiding gloom.

Every few steps he had to stop and peer ahead. He forced himself to caution, terrified of getting lost or trapped in some hole - his chance to get to Creggan before Silas, forever gone. And always there, the nightmare image of the man swooping from the sky to hurt Katriana haunted him. How could he have brought such misery on the girl and her father? He pushed on, concentrating every effort on moving forward.

He was fighting through waist-high thorns when some tipping point - a coincidence of blocked moon, thick clouds, nearby trees and tiredness - caused the world around him to vanish as though he had just donned a black sack over his head.

It pressed on his face and physically pushed him back so that he had to sway to find his balance.

Something, probably a bat, swooped close to his ear. Tom tumbled backwards in fright, his clothes clawed by hooks, a thousand curved thorns grappling him to the ground, refusing to let him go until they had bled him. When he gained his feet, he cursed the black pit that had swallowed the night. He could no longer see the subtle shades of black outlining the curve of the hill and the infernal bracken became a malevolent infestation, stinging and stabbing, taunting and clinging. He tried looking askance as he'd done with the deer so very long ago but the night was thick and fat and fast and as impenetrable as the malicious bush gripping him. Stretching his arms, he felt his way ahead, fingers tipping lightly over the dense vegetation.

This action - his arms outstretched through black air - reminded him of his experience in the cave and immediately, on making the connection, Tom sensed a strange glow from everything around him, as though the grass, the trees, the mountains and the ground itself had suddenly acquired the gift of light. It was faint at first but Tom recognised the effect immediately. He did not understand how it was happening but at this point he did not care.

Around him - everywhere - the land turned luminescent. He focused on whatever detail lurched his way, trying to sharpen the effect in his mind. The light was a faint blue but, to his right, a hint of green soon formed itself into the strangest looking tree he had ever seen. It was blurred, deliberately it seemed, as though its maker had yet to decide its exact shape. Around him, the thorns became a smoky brown mass, wafting back and forth, anchored and blown by a shifting, slow-mo breeze.

He had not heard it before, but now the sound of running water gurgled through the brightening scenery.

The world he looked upon was not some strange sketch but a tangible reality where directly in front of him, a kilometre from where he stood, the mountain drifted out of the darkness and presented itself to him, the undulating ground to his right, solid and now bright as a day lit from within.

Above, a cloudless night sky glittered with black satin sequins.

He looked to his left and his heart leapt with sudden excitement.

No more than twenty metres away, a ghostly fence cut the ground. To its right, the bloody thorns, to its left, a camp site and then a shaven lawn so massive that Tom knew before he saw the smoky flags, that the smooth carpeted landscape was that of a golf course. Ignoring the pain, his shredded clothes, he battled back the way he came, skirted the thorns and made for the fence on easy ground.

He stared at the waist-high wire. It ran from fuzzy post to fuzzy post. Tom inched his hand down towards the horizontal line, fearful that the thing might slice his fingers.

When he felt nothing at the point of touch, or rather the point of no-touch, the hazy linear smudge dropped a fraction, repelled it seemed by his skin. He continued chasing the ghostly barrier for a further half-hand and then, at last, when he began to think it would sink to the ground, found the solid object he knew had to be there. The line stopped moving, solidified and thinned. He ran his fingers left and right, recognising the smooth slide of clean wire. The smoky haze continued to coalesce, changing colour as it did until the line became unmistakably metallic. Tom stretched one leg and then another over the fence and felt the smooth cultivated turf under his feet. If he had not been so worried about Katriana and her father, the boy would have cried for joy. Instead, he looked ahead, saw the unmistakable scar running across the hill and headed as fast as his sanity would let him, towards it.

Tom was amazed how quickly he became accustomed to the weird environment that surrounded him. He grew bolder with each minute so that when he found a small footbridge crossing a stream, he did not stop to test the platform for safety or even reality, but bounded across the thing in five leaping strides. He barely noticed the water flowing from right to left under his feet, its presence highlighted by shimmering eddies, wispy groups of dark and pale-blue, swirling and bubbling softly towards the sea.

At last, after vaulting a high fence, Tom jumped onto a track which, even in the midst of surreality, he immediately recognised as the connecting link between road and footpath from his journey to the village.

He picked up his speed and ran and ran and ran.

When he reached the saddle summit, he stood on the crest and caught his breath, sweat and blood and mud covering his wretched body. He desperately needed to stop, to recover for two minutes before running down the other side, but he could not afford the time.

Heart and breath and feet pounding, he careered, almost beyond control, towards his old home and fifteen minutes later, he looked down on Creggan's roof. A confused emotional mash-up threatened to make him shout for joy, cry in sorrow and scream an angry challenge to the world to leave her alone.

There, in the bright glow of lamplight, standing on the rock - their rock - Katriana peered up the hill, blind to his presence. Tom bolted down the slope towards her.

FORTY EIGHT

Tom had no illusions that their reunion would be a happy one but still, Katriana's fury shocked him. Exhausted and driven by mixed emotions, the boy's windblown tears became tears of rage.

'We haven't got time for this,' he yelled.

When she had first seen Tom stumbling towards her, the girl's voice sung with hope. She ran to him, ready to embrace but stopped suddenly and looked beyond him. 'Where are they?'

'I'll explain later,' Tom replied. 'Where's your father?'

He moved towards the cottage, its whitewashed walls brilliant against the night but Katriana, black hair flying wildly, spun him on the spot, her eyes sudden slits of anger. 'Where is everyone, Tom?'

Tom hesitated, torn between a need to explain and the torture of awful expectation.

'There's no rescue, Katriana. We need to get out of here.'

Katriana's fingers locked on Tom's arm, nails digging deep through his sleeve reminding him of the thorns he had so recently escaped. He understood her anger, felt it to his core and fought its destructive force. 'My.... father. Silas. He's here!'

'Do the police know about us?'

'He's mad.'

'The police, Tom. Is help coming?'

Tom shook himself free and grasped the girl by the shoulders. 'Listen to me, Katriana. 'I tried to get help, but Silas - the man in the boat - he's here. He's on his way.'

Katriana pulled away, looking alternately up the hill, out to sea and back to the cottage, the night an unbroken wall of misery surrounding them.

'You're sick! There's no-one?'

Tom's fury needed a target. He struggled against his anger, tried to direct it to action.

He turned and ran to the door, the girl on his heels, spinning him in fury as he fumbled the handle.

Tom exploded. He pushed her hard. 'We've no time for this,' he yelled. Katriana staggered back and Tom's wretched emotions swung wildly so that he almost stopped what he was doing and went to her. Instead, as the girl fought her balance, Tom took the lamp and bolted into the cottage.

On the surface, Calum's condition had hardly changed but Tom could tell that he was close to death - his breathing shallow, skin white, delirium gone.

Katriana - suddenly there again - flew at Tom, striking his face hard with an open hand.

He grabbed her, spun and pinned her arms, hugging her back to him. As she struggled, Tom fought the urge to hit her. He just wanted to help. He felt so guilty. Why was she doing this?

'I have something for him,' he said through gritted teeth.

Katriana did not seem to hear, her head swinging left and right, her hair whipping his face.

'He's dying, Katriana. Your father's dying.'

The girl seemed to deflate. She sank to her knees, the hiss of the lamp like leaking air. Tom dropped with her.

'He can't die. He can't.'

Together on the floor, Tom hugged her back, eased the pressure on her arms.

'You have to trust me. I can help him.'

She sat motionless, streaked and glittering cheeks, moist, red-rimmed eyes fixed on her father. Tom left her on the floor and hurried to the kitchen. Moments later he returned with a small pot of cold water and placed it on the table beside the bed. Katriana had moved to her father's side. She held his hand, tears flowing, shoulders shaking uncontrollably. She watched the boy with suspicion but said nothing.

Tom removed the small phial from his pocket. He had no idea if the serum would work, how much to use or if he would need multiple treatments.

Careful to preserve every drop, the boy peeled the duvet to reveal Calum's bloated leg. He heaved from the stench, a sweet mix of rotten meat and bananas. Gagging his revulsion, he unscrewed the top and dripped, one, two, three, four drops of liquid onto the worst area of the man's leg.

Turning to Katriana, he said. 'A knife. I need a knife.'

She stared at him as though he was speaking a foreign language, but then suddenly rose and went to the kitchen.

Tom took the knife from her hands and turned his attention to the leg.

'My God!' Katriana looked at the bubbling mass of puss spreading from the spots where Tom had dropped the serum. The effect was that of a corrosive acid and not a soothing balm.

'I know it looks bad but I've seen it work.' He turned, noting her distress, delaying the moment he had to use the knife.

'I need a glass of water,' he said. 'Cold.'

Katriana did as she was told and as she left the room, Tom quickly dug the knife into the swollen bag of black and green fluid that was Calum's leg. He winced as a torrent of mush spurted over his face and flooded the bed. Fighting the vomit rising in his own stomach, Tom dripped a few more drops, this time into the wound he had created. As he prised the putrid flesh apart with finger and thumb, two halves of bone crunched, one over the other, the grinding sound somehow running through his own bones and landing on his teeth.

'What are you doing?'

Katriana stood at his side, her face twisted in horror. She grabbed the knife from the boy and swung her hand back to strike. Tom leapt to his feet, catching her wrist mid-stab. Without thinking he twisted her arm, the weapon clunking to the floor. He held her fast, turning them both to look at her father.

Still bubbling and cracking his flesh, there was now an unmistakable change in the appearance of the leg close to the places Tom had administered the first splashes of serum. Katriana saw this too and Tom felt the fight leave her.

Much as he wanted to stay with her, to watch the miracle unfold, Tom had things to do.

He placed the phial into the girl's hands. 'Put three drops in the glass and try to get him to drink it.'

She nodded her head, transfixed by the macabre scene before her.

Tom picked up the second lamp and moved to the hall. He threw open the cupboard under the stairs and ploughed through its contents. By the time he had chosen the crowbar, the hallway was littered with junk. Pieces of wood, empty tins, a splattered cloth, a sledge hammer and a jumble of rock-hard brushes lay unwanted at his back.

He had thought of using the hammer, but it was heavy, too unwieldy. He swung the crowbar, getting the sense of its weight, its potential for damage. Satisfied, he clambered over the scrapheap and entered the room he and Katriana had shared only yesterday. He did not know what he was looking for. They had to leave as soon as they could. There was no way they could carry Calum and there was no boat to ferry him out. They would have to stay put until he could walk, but broken bone was not torn flesh. Would it work?

These thoughts plagued him as he searched for anything that might help them get out of there alive.

He was rummaging through a drawer of old keys and jigsaw bits when Katriana appeared at his back and closed the door quietly behind her.

She was calmer now but the urgency and despair were still there.

'I want to know what's going on, Tom.'

Tom's instinct was to keep searching. They had to prepare for the worst but his confidence in finding something he could use was fading fast. He turned to speak and as the words formed in his mind, he caught his breath and froze.

There, to Katriana's right, was Kathleen, her ghostly image bloodied, her dress torn, hair dishevelled. Tom's eye was drawn to her neck, to the heart stone. His hand drifted to his pocket and he felt it there, solid and comforting

'What's wrong, Tom?' said Katriana. But her voice was drowned by Kathleen's anguished cry.

'Get out, Tom. Get out while you still can.'

And as she said it, the door exploded behind her and Silas took her place, his cruel smile as real as Katriana's shocked expression as she lay bleeding and helpless on the floor.

FORTY NINE

Silas walked through the splintered door holding the sledgehammer. He stopped at Katriana's prostrate body, eyes wide, feet apart - a movie poster in hell. He stood erect, apparently fit, but his left cheek was ripped open extending a strange lop-sided smile to his ear.

'You're clever, boy. Foolish, but clever.'

Kathleen was gone and Tom hesitated, cradling the crowbar opposite the shattered door. The man seemed to vibrate, an overstressed machine about to blow, his neck a bulbous trapezoid, sinuous, sloping struts visibly tensed, carotid pulse pacing a hate-filled heart.

'You found my little gift.'

Tom stepped forward to look at Katriana and groaned inwardly at the red stain on her outstretched arm.

'Stop!' Silas swung the hammer over his head in a lazy curve and held it suspended over the girl's face. 'She's alive. For now.' His cheek was hideous and blood burbled from the gash as he spoke, his moving lips ripping apart a closing wound. Tom was surprised by this. Had the serum run its course? If the man had gashed himself in the accident, surely it should have healed by now.

He stopped, noting the tension running up Silas' arms to the wooden shaft, shaking the hammer as though fed by ten thousand volts.

'Touch her and I'll kill you,' said Tom.

Silas' laugh was insane and brief. It was followed by a grotesque sneer.

'You've had many, many years to do that, boy and I'm still here.'

He looked from Tom to the girl. 'You have a choice. I kill the girl, then I kill you.'

That terrible, corrupted grin. 'Or you can help me.'

'I'll help,' Tom said.

'You never could get the hang of lying.'

Tom imagined himself springing for Silas, mentally gauging the time to reach him against the deadly swing of the hammer.

'Drop the bar.'

Tom did as he was told.

'Move to the far wall,' he said. 'Good boy.' His voice was a mockery of praise. 'Spread your arms and lean forward.... Feet out .. Further.'

Tom, his forehead touching the wall, body angled like a badly placed ladder, was suddenly surprised to feel Silas' breath on his neck. He had crossed the room in complete silence.

'I owe you, boy,' he whispered.

Something exploded in his kidneys as the handle of Silas' hammer slammed into his back. His legs folded and everything turned black as he crashed to the floor.

*

Tom's feet were freezing. He was back in Silas' underground den and what he saw when he awoke brought the full horror of their situation to him. A rush of unwanted memories erupted in his head - dark satanic visions created and destroyed, consumed by one another in an escalating race to capture his sanity.

He sat in a chair. *The* chair. Numb feet dipped in cold water, wrists and ankles strapped to rotten wood. Beside him Katriana, her head slumped sideways, her hair a threaded veil half covering her face, was perfectly still.

Tom felt the harsh dig of metal on the back of his neck and, like a cup of honey in hell, Katriana's warm hand bound to his.

Movement was difficult under the strap binding his forehead but there was no power running through the connection and by straining every muscle in his neck, he watched the girl for signs of life, saw their hands, clasped and bound with black tape.

He squeezed, gently at first, and then tighter, but sensed no reaction. It was obvious however, by the soft warmth flowing between them that the girl was still alive.

A noise beyond the open archway drew Tom's attention to the

main chamber. Silas was somewhere close. The cavern was lit by a single gas lamp that Tom guessed had come from the cottage. Its incandescent glow bounced around the walls, spreading its light surprisingly well throughout.

A fleeting, ill-defined shadow brushed the floor beyond the archway. Silas was busy. How long before the man would return, Tom did not know, but he had to assume that it would be seconds, not minutes. He wasted little time trying to free himself, checking only briefly the security of his bonds. He strained to see Katriana, considered whispering her name but it was obvious, even from his limited viewpoint that she was out cold.

Tom thought of Silas then, tried to figure his next move. The man needed Tom. He'd always needed him. But Tom could figure no way to leverage this fact. He could try, of course. Tell the madman that he'd get nothing from Tom if he didn't set the girl free. But Tom knew it was an empty threat. While Silas had Katriana, the boy would do as he was told, just like he had when the creature of his childhood had tormented his mother. Tom did not notice his reversion to thinking of Kathleen as his mother. In all that mattered, that's exactly who she was.

Tom understood that if he was to defeat Silas, he had to get inside the man's head.

Inside his head.

Just as he had back in the lab. He cast back to the moment Silas had shown him Tess' anguish, remembered the link all those years ago in this very cave. He thought of the visions, the knowledge of future and past and, Katriana's hand in his, he remembered the beauty by his side as he had shared a few loving memories with his family. Katriana had been there with him, in spirit at least. In the cottage, watching him dance with his mother. Running alongside Tom and Tess on the beach. Sharing his memories.

Inside his head.

Unaware he was doing it, Tom cleared his mind, the world faded away and another part of him floated free, looking down at the couple locked together in helpless captivity.

Tom looked at their hands, felt the bond, saw her life in his grip and drifted down again, drawn to her. This part of Tom closed his fingers around the girl's and joined with her in a way that seemed as natural to the boy as breathing.

Unaware he had done so, Silas had opened the boy to his gift more fully than even Tom had realised.

Until now.

Tom took his mind to the top of a mountain. He recognised its jagged peak, the loch and sea at its feet.

And he knew its name.

Corven.

He whispered to the surrounding air. 'Katriana.'

The girl, as Tom knew she would, appeared at his side.

She looked at him with dreamy, dark eyes and drew close. Tom opened his arms and enfolded her, the beauty of their surroundings matched only by that of the moment.

Tom looked at Katriana, her hair once again shining black, her clothing clean, her skin perfect, her eyes untroubled.

He held her, and she held him. Tom realised that Katriana thought the dream was hers alone. He kept her close, felt the softness of her, the peace of ignorant sleep. He drank her presence and prepared to tell her what she needed to know, to bring her back to the hell she'd only just escaped.

FIFTY

Sleepy white clouds drifted in the high breeze. A bright blue sky patched the gaps and the sun came and went through lazy shadows.

Corven, its summit a small table of sloping rock on a massive pillar, was surrounded by mountain and sea. Either side, a string of peaks was threaded together by a steep rocky ridge. Giddy slopes dropped to secluded blue lochans that twinkled bright and pretty in the folds of tortured rock.

'I want to show you something,' said Tom. He turned to the sea, Katriana silent by his side. Neither boy nor girl flinched as a large sphere, suddenly there, drew towards them with slow intelligent purpose. Its surface, if such a thing can be described so, was an intangible play of convoluted, shifting colours - transparent as glass, solid as air.

Katriana was dreaming, the strange sight an unquestioned fact that needed no explanation.

Standing on the mountain, wrapped in a world of imagined substance, imagined words and imagined time, Tom felt no need to hurry or bludgeon the girl's tranquil fantasy. She believed what she saw. Everything was dream-time normal.

'This is how I got here. How I travel.'

The sphere, closer and closer, filled their vision, forming and conforming to the surrounding rock so that its centre remained clean and untouched by the world through which it moved.

So much was returning to Tom, so much waited for him to explore. He now recognised the mountain, understood its significance, but his priorities were with Katriana, in finding a way out.

He took her then, with the disjointed efficiency of thought, to his birthing cliff by Creggan, replayed those snatched moments of life he had so far recovered.

'This is a dream,' said Katriana.

Tom eased her towards reality. 'A dream, yes.' He took her hand. 'But not all dreams are false,' he said.

And then, watching events at Creggan, Tom tried to skirt the memory of her father's fate, but Katriana suddenly stiffened and Tom knew that her pain was too powerful, too important, to ignore. Her journey towards the nightmare had begun.

Watching Calum struggle, Tom tried to keep the sound of cracking bone from his mind but heard it just the same, shared it reluctantly with the broken man's daughter. They moved on, Tom lingering over the healing serum applied to his arm and then to Calum's leg, labouring on the hope he prayed it would bring to her.

By the time he was finished, Katriana, in her dream, understood all that Tom had given her. Their thoughts entwined, Tom realised that Katriana's blind acceptance of the dream was not the same as true belief, but in the brief connection of minds, he was preparing her for what was to come - for a moment when explanations took time, when the only thing that mattered is how - and how fast - they acted together.

He showed her the rescue helicopter, the photograph of his sister, Silas' house, the lab, the old man's transformation.

And then at last, steeling himself for the deadly connection between now and then, he let her share an instant with him in the cubicle, the white flies, the bubbling skin, the acid pain, his bizarre escape - that same trick, the power he needed to recall now - a journey through time that could kill her as surely as the man who held them there.

In the logic of the dream, Katriana accepted Tom's answer when she asked what had happened.

'We're from the future. Tess, Silas and me.'

They stood atop the mountain again. The coloured orb awaiting his unspoken command.

'My sister and I... we're... different from others. We travel unharmed. Protected by that.' He pointed to the object before them. 'Silas cannot.'

'Then why did he do it? Why risk his life to bring you to Arran all those years ago?' Katriana could have been talking about an airsick passenger on a trans-globe flight.

Tom dug deep but found nothing. 'I don't know.'

But despite the speed of their transaction, time was still ticking in the cavern.

He started to explain what he intended to do. 'The Earth rotates,' he told her. 'It journeys through space, through the galaxy and through the universe.'

A faint noise, beyond the world he had created, barely reached him through his focus on the girl.

'People wondered for centuries why no one has visited them from the future. But they have.'

Katriana, her father coming and going in her thoughts, nodded her head with distracted interest.

'They all died and no-one knew why until a man called Peter Smith pointed out the obvious. You cannot travel in time alone. From one second to another, the place you were moves.' As he spoke, they both imagined Tom's cubicle-prison spin away from him, the boy's body shifting in time, remaining motionless as the chair, the lab and the Earth itself continued its journey without him. As Tom reviewed what had happened, he was struck by the notion that he had made the tiny leap in time without the aid or protection from the sphere, a feat he knew should have killed him. 'I can do it again,' he started to say, but before he could finish the thought, Silas' voice, and a slap across Tom's face, shattered Corven, mountain and sea – disconnected his secret union with Katriana.

'Wake up, boy.'

Silas seemed to glow in the reflected light of the lamp, his bald head a beacon with eyes.

To his left, Katriana flinched, a sudden extended moan filling the cavern.

'Oh, this brings back so many memories.'

Tom squeezed Katriana's hand, tried to comfort her without taking his eyes from Silas.

He had to act quickly. Silas was ready. Somewhere, locked deep and safe, the memories that had so far eluded him, rose closer to the light. He instinctively looked at Silas' hand and saw the thing he dreaded. The small rod, innocent as a horse whip, deadly as a cattle prod, pointed down, tapping lightly against his lower leg.

Tom was not frightened of the weapon for his own sake. For him, there was worse to come. But the rod, for some reason akin to sentimentality, was Silas' favourite tool of pain, the one he had used on the boy's mother. Tom believed it brought Silas closer to the power he yielded - an intimate connection between him and his victim.

Silas raised the tip and ran it lightly across Katriana's cheek

'Here's what we do, boy.'

Tom strained to watch the girl. Still unconscious, her head pushed into the back of the chair, a reflex action to escape the menace intruding into her dream.

'I am going to join you now and we're going to leave here together.'

Tom tried to calm his voice. He had to keep control of his thoughts. 'It'll kill you.'

'I survived.'

Tom noted the shudder run through Silas' body as both he and the boy remembered the awful shape the man had been in when they had arrived at Creggan over a century ago.

'There was no help here. Medicine was primitive. That won't be the case on the other side.' His fingers tightened around the handle, a precursor, Tom knew, to the shocking stab of current that could leap from its tip.

Tom tried to distract him.

'If I do this, you'll leave her alone?'

Silas smiled his horrible smile, his teeth stained with his own blood. 'Why would we take her?'

'What if I can't do it?'

'There are many ways this could end, I doubt that's one you'd like.'

'What about Tess?'

Silas ignored his question. 'We are going to join - all three of us. I'll know every thought you think, every action before you take it.'

As he spoke, Silas removed the rod from Katriana's face, collapsed it and stowed it on his belt. He took his own seat, leaned forward and reached out, left and right hands to either side of the girl and boy, completing the triangle, closing the circuit that would bind them together for what was yet to come.

'Remember, boy. I don't have the patience I once had. I *will* kill her.'

Tom had no doubt that Silas spoke the truth. He felt the bony hand cover his bound wrist, the touch more repugnant than ever. He had no choice. If he took him away from here, Katriana and her father would be safe.

But as he prepared to do as he was told, a billion voices, somehow entangled with the thoughts he dredged from that deep place, screamed in terror and Tom squirmed in his seat, trying to push them away, to concentrate on nothing but what he had to do.

A voice, Silas', boomed in his head and at the same moment the chair, the brace at the back of his neck, jolted to life. The sound pushed the cacophony down, suppressed the mass of humanity crying, pleading for his help.

'They're no concern of yours, Tom. They're sinners. It's time.'

With Silas in his thoughts, Tom pushed the voices away. He sensed Katriana join them, felt the anguish flow through her and into him. He had to be strong. He had to keep his secrets from Silas. Compartmentalise. He forced himself to give the man what he wanted, to keep him happy until he was ready. At every moment, his thoughts and plans threatened to surface and he forced them down and down, bringing the image of their journey to the future to the front, distracting him with visions of success.

In this mindset, splitting his personality in two, he swung to action.

FIFTY ONE

They stood atop Corven, the same clouds, the same drifting shadows, the same gut-churning cliffs.

Silas and Tom looked at each other, enmity flowing between them like poison gas.

'Bring the girl.'

Tom wanted to separate them, to sublimate Katriana to another compartment he could work on in secret, bury his link to her in his subconscious. But Silas was adamant and refusing him would look suspicious.

Katriana drifted into view. She looked from Tom to the man beside her, eyes popping, nostrils flaring. She threw herself at him, fingers clawed, ready to rip another hole in his face. Silas simply vanished and reappeared on the peak directly behind her.

'Control the witch or I'll do it for you.'

Tom placed a hand on the girl's shoulder, felt her hatred mingle with his. 'We'll be gone soon. You'll be safe.'

Silas butted in, not with words but with an image he projected to the pair, an image that explained what he expected to happen next.

In that image, Tom, Katriana and Silas looked at themselves floating in a giant square in the sky, a screen with no substance, as real as the mountain they stood on.

Through and within that strange detached window, they sat in the cavern, boy and girl bound to each other, their faces twisted in anguish. Silas, his disfigured expression inscrutable, suddenly grinned and a second later disappeared with Tom from the chair. As they did, Katriana's bound hand became free and she awoke. She could now go to her father, get help. The message was clear - no words needed. Tom and Silas would never be seen again in her lifetime. It was a powerful statement.

But, as Tom watched, his outward appearance defeated, he struggled to hide his suppressed thoughts. Deep in some locked chamber the sinners screamed a collective wail of despair, drowning him in inconsolable sadness, swamping him with a sense that in doing as he was told, he was somehow condemning them to a pitiless, infinite hell. He squashed the destructive cacophony, tried to smile at the girl, told her, in thought, that she would be OK. Everything would be fine.

Tom turned to the sea and prepared to conjure the sphere. But as he did, a cloud, unlike its fluffy neighbours, caught his attention. Darker, it moved against the breeze, flowing its own course, swooping this way and that as though alive. If he hadn't seen it before, the cloud could have been a curious artefact of the dream-world he'd created to link the trio together. But Tom understood it perfectly. Hour by hour, fact by fact, a snatch of meaning here, a sudden insight there, the fog of his life's journey lifted. He recognised the artefact and saw in it an opportunity - a diversion that could buy him the time he needed to reconcile his conscience with his desire to save the girl. He turned his attention to the cloud, noting as he did, that Silas did not flinch. He'd expected nothing less. Looking at the thing, it drew towards them, its substance breaking to tiny dots and then growing in size to become an enormous flock that hugged itself and turned and dived as one; birds of the strangest hue that, to Tom, seemed as normal as the land.

Closer, closer, they took shape, formed themselves to words, familiar words - Dreamwords. With these symbols he could control everything, retrieve memories lost, recall maps, a quadrillion facts and figures, images, sounds and smells. He imagined his destination and it came to him, figures circling his head until he reached out and grasped the collective with his left hand. Katriana looked on, puzzled but silent.

The symbols Tom selected were not words. They were numbers.

2999

As Tom's fingers curled around the circling date, it stopped, its brown surface now a melting red, spreading over his hand, his arm, engulfing him. Corven, the sky, mountain and sea, disappeared, replaced by a black void, a universe where the objects surrounding them were not planets and stars but clusters of light that seemed to shine internally, swooping this way and that, each group a colour;

blues, reds, yellows and oranges.

Tom did not need to do this. He wasn't like the others. He alone could control the sphere by simply deciding to do so, but he remembered Silas' endless instructions. This is how it should be done. *Use Dreamwords, boy. That's what it's for.*

Edinburgh Castle.

This was their destination in that far future. This was Home for Silas. Tom imagined the words and from a distant constellation they flew at him – first the E and then the D, followed in quick succession by the others as they made Tom's thought whole. They circled Tom's upper body until the boy on the mountain-top reached out and drew them all; Katriana, Tom and Silas, towards their ultimate goal.

Tom did all this as an automaton. An accountant accessing a spreadsheet. Click, click, click.

But Silas was transfixed, his expectation rising with each step, Katriana calmly accepting whatever came her way.

And all the while, beneath the automotive actions, Tom's subconscious, his other self, snatched at brief insights, alternative actions, moulding his plan until he could almost taste it.

Before the physical leap in time, Tom brought the image of their supposed destination to their minds, as though setting aim for the 'jump'. Floating high over a dark castle, the clouds above them scudded swarms of living words. A theatrical slight of hand, a visual decoy in the dreamscape of Corven they now occupied: Tom brought the sphere closer and closer still.

Big enough to hold Silas and the boy, it drifted slowly towards the mountain as they stood on its summit.

As it neared, and before he allowed the thing to engulf them, Tom turned to Katriana, reached out and clasped her hands in his. They embraced, the hate and bile consuming them suddenly gone. Tom sensed an unformed thought in Katriana's mind. *Don't go*, it whispered. But she forced it down, killed it at birth.

'Bring her,' the man said.

The pair of them looked at Silas in surprise, the icy breath of evil freezing the precious moment to a frigid and awkward silence. The distraction was enough for Tom to lose the focus on suppressing his thoughts. It was only for a moment but in communion with Katriana, she suddenly felt that fear. Not for Tom himself but for *them*. Strangers. So many of them. The despair of a billion frightened people. She gasped in shock at the enormity of the secret held tight within the boy's muffled thoughts

They broke contact, Silas' cruel smile an indication that he had misconstrued her reaction.

'Stay, go. I could care less.'

He grasped Tom by the arm and turned him away from the girl. Tom let his grip fall, his world suddenly devoid of meaning.

But as the sphere closed on Silas and Tom, Katriana threw herself at the boy, wrapping her arms around his neck, tears of frustration, confusion tearing her apart. At her touch, Tom knew that she understood there was more to this than the lives of four people, understood that they had to fight, understood too that in doing so they might lose the small victory of life they appeared to have won.

No words were exchanged and once more Silas was preoccupied by his short-term goals, the notion of self-sacrifice too removed from his current state to register that what he witnessed was anything more than the selfishness of parting love.

'Touching,' he mocked.

The sphere closed around them, Katriana suddenly alone.

Tom had decided what to do but he did not voice the decision to himself, pushed it from the upper reaches of self they all shared.

To take a thousand-year journey with the girl could kill her but, as Silas said, where they intended to go, medicine could save her. She could live. They could live together. But what of Katriana's father or the sinners crying for help?

So! He would take her. He would bring Silas. All three would travel together. Not, however, exactly as the man had ordered. As the glimmer of a smile spread over Silas' lips, Tom reached through the shimmering bubble and grasped Katriana's arm. He pulled hard, drawing her to him and in the same instant, as he felt Silas dig his fingernails into his bound wrist in the real world of the cave, he could sense him stand, the fingers suddenly slack, the link in the chair about to be broken.

But Tom knew it was too late. They were moving – wrapped inside the protective bubble underground - and there was nothing the monster holding them could do about it.

FIFTY TWO

The transit was brief and only Tom was truly prepared for the sudden dislocation they all felt.

Sitting there in the cavern, the dreamers opened their eyes at the same time. The hiss of the lamp vanished, the chairs, the pool at their feet, the straps on their wrists and ankles, all plunged backwards and down.

Tom prayed he'd got it right. Too short and they would be buried underground, too long and they could find themselves thousands of feet in the air. He did not navigate the route in terms of time but pictured where he wanted to be, brought the spot to focus as he grabbed the girl, and some part of him, as instinctive and invisible as the mechanism of his beating heart, set the sphere, calculated the temporal coordinates and launched the journey into space and time. For such a short trip, he prayed the swirling bubble of light would protect Katriana from harm.

Hopping between brief gaps in time, they touched nothing and nothing touched them. A span of seconds split to an infinite string of tiny jumps, each a frozen instant of zero, threaded to a smooth curve that was measured in moments - not the centuries Silas had ordered.

The cavern plummeted. Walls and roof like wisps of thought, fled them. And then they were outside. Everything fast, no room for error, a thousand ways to die.

Silas, continuing his break from the circuit, pulled his hand free as the Earth rotated and stopped. The ruin, Creggan, a single 60 watt bulb glowing through the window, the faint wash of white surf at the water's edge, the sea itself.

And for the briefest instant, in the transition between imaginary time and the world they lived in, the trio seemed to hang above the water as though catching gravity by surprise. And then, snatched from the air, they fell, the savage pull of Earth absolute and ruthless. Tom kicked out at Silas, missing his head and smashing his shoulder. Katriana, her hand now loosely taped to his, cried in sudden fright. Kicking out thus, the boy pushed himself back, slamming hard into the girl, but Silas took the brunt of the brutal thud.

The protective bubble gone, Tom spun as he fell.

Closest to the shore, Katriana and Tom heard Silas scream in fury as he realised he'd been tricked.

Falling, falling - Tom looked down.

It was instinct. A mistake.

He looked down and the world smashed him in the face.

The relief of discovering he was close to where he wanted to be was crushed as his twisted body hit the water.

His free hand broke the surface first, followed by his right hip and then his face.

Whap!

It was as though someone had smashed his eyes with two perfectly fitting squash balls. He fought to stay conscious, water engulfing them. Down and down they went, blind, Tom's eyes bleeding in the dark. When they finally hit the bottom, the punch of the fall was gone. Tom pushed up, the ascent a long life of bursting lungs. The muffled gurgle of bubble and surf disappeared as they surfaced.

Katriana, a heavy doll tied to his wrist, suddenly came alive. She lashed out in terror and confusion. Tom had prepared the girl as much as he could but ultimately she was lost, dragged from nightmare to nightmare, drowning now in a mass of black fluid, a sea of ink that had miraculously replaced mountain and castle.

She thrashed her arms, jerking Tom towards her, the tape holding them together like loving cuffs. They were close to the shore, closer than Tom had hoped and it was only by luck that they missed the rock that had sent the dingy to the bottom in that fateful, long-ago, storm.

Entangled and almost blind, they sank again

Dark as it was outside, it was darker still underwater. The tide was out but not far enough and his feet found nothing but a shard of wood that could have been part of the shattered boat.

He wrapped his free arm around the girl and kicked upwards again, sensed the change in her as she came to grips with where she was. Slowly, they calmed themselves and tread water.

Barely feet away, Silas splashed towards them. Suddenly synchronised, the pair swam to the sound of the surf, heading for the jumble of rocks jutting into the water, pulling themselves hand over hand across its barnacled face, searching for a way to climb from the sea.

Silas drove in from their left, pushing them around the wrong side of the rock, away from the cottage. Closer to the shore now, the swell hefted them upwards and down in deceptively gentle waves that crashed ten metres away against the shore. Difficult as it was to see, Tom knew from countless childhood swims that he was being pushed towards a cul-de-sac. He listened to the sea whoosh-and-swirl, in and out of the v-shaped trap. There was one spot they might climb, a small bulge jutting from the outcrop they now skirted. Alone, he could scale it with difficulty but tethered to the girl, he was not so sure.

'Wait,' said Tom. Katriana clung to the rock, gasping for breath. Listening.

For Tom, activating the map turned out to be simple. Eyes open or eyes closed, the world became a surreal, game-maker's dream.

The rock shone an eerie bright blue, the night sky alive with moon and stars, all perfectly positioned for the time and place. Up to their chests in water, the view was limited, but it was the sea itself where the strangeness of the effect was most striking. Although the sky was a bejewelled black, the overall scene was of a strange daylight. Where he could see beyond the rocks, the grassy mountain behind Creggan shone green and brown, the landscape familiar and vaguely comforting.

The sea was a dark wash of amorphous blue, a deep blue that could have matched the sky with a little more effort. It rose as it lifted them, smoky, continually updating itself to the best guess possible, helped, Tom was sure, by his hearing, the touch of his wet clothes and body and the up-and-down motion of the couple clinging to the reference-frame of the rock.

Real and unreal meshed almost to perfection. The immersive map was a Godsend. The rock, drawn perhaps from the recall of youthful adventures, was detailed enough to reveal the shelf that was to be their exit ramp. Beside him, Katriana's face was striking, her beauty hardly diminished by the bruise his mind placed above her eye or the blood on her arm. Only her position was blurred. But right then, tethered to Tom, she was helpless, tragic and lost

Behind them, Silas closed the gap. He was almost invisible, a vague but closing smudge that spread over a large area 20 metres to their left. But as they splashed and clawed their way around the outcrop, Tom was surprised to note that Silas' frantic thrash was suddenly fading. Miraculously, it seemed, he had missed them in the dark and instead swam directly for shore.

Now, razor shells cutting their fingers, they clung to the shelf as it rose and fell with the pulse of heaving water.

'We have to free our hands,' whispered Tom.

Over time, Tom noticed that with his eyes open, tiny details plucked from the gloom of normal vision overlaid and sharpened the world-view fed to his mind. And thus, black hair streaked Katriana's face like cracks through skin.

She nodded, coughing salt water as she clung to the rock to steady herself.

Facing each other, their clasped hands outward, Tom brought the tape to his teeth and ripped at its edges. Tangy salt swamped his mouth and, choking back a lungful of liquid, he wormed at the thing until the edge tore - no more than a fraction at first - and then, under pressure from their constant movement, widened and ripped.

'He'll go to the cottage,' said Tom.

'I need to get to my father.'

Gaining ground was easier than the boy had expected. Timing it perfectly to the swell, he scrabbled up the outcrop. Kneeling, he hauled Katriana onto the shelf and together, as silent as their dripping clothes and laboured breathing would allow, they turned to the cottage in the distance.

The door was open, its rectangle of light spilling carelessly onto the dark grass in front.

He crouched down. Katriana followed.

Tom was about to suggest going in alone to check things out when they heard her father's cry.

'Katriana. Katriana,' he yelled.

Katriana opened her mouth to reply but Tom stopped her, his hand gentle on her lips, her breath surprisingly hot.

Ahead, a hazy Golamesque presence flitted among the rocks. As soon as he saw it, Tom knew it wasn't Calum. The movement was sly, sleekit, slimy.

And dangerous.

He had no idea if the man knew they were there but they could take no chances. It was just possible, if they could escape his notice, they would be able to get to the cottage before he did.

But as Tom thought this out, the vapour that was Silas suddenly rose, solidifying to a brutal silhouette framed by the cottage, a black devil rising from the grave.

Katriana yelled in fright and suddenly, without warning, her father, his voice a rumbling menace roared from a spot behind the man.

'Move away from her.'

Silas sprung round at the sound of the man's voice - the man who was supposed to be crippled or dead.

Calum was huge. He limped badly, scarcely able to stand on the injured leg, but he was mobile. Alive.

Alive and every bit the giant he ever was.

FIFTY THREE

They outnumbered Silas three to one, but some instinct, some Pavlovian program, told Tom to assume nothing.

Indistinct in the blue glow, he saw the swift movement of brown on brown, the shapeless but definite snap of an arm lashing forward towards Calum.

'Look out!' Tom yelled.

But his voice was lost, drowned by a terrible cry from the man trying to help them.

A flash, a crack of light, ripped through Tom's map. Lightning arced from the glowing tip of Silas' steel rod, scorching the side of Calum's face. Everything around them - the rocks, Katriana, Silas and the foul creature itself - was transformed in a series of rapid flashes. Tom's map was swamped by the intensity of the sudden light and died.

Calum seemed to leap backwards, a succession of stop-motion photos. He plunged into the sea. Katriana screamed and Tom, blinded now by tiny forks breeding behind his eyelids, took a wild guess at Silas' position. He charged, feet solid on razor rock.

Enraged, Silas turned to confront the boy. He raised the rod to strike but was too late.

Tom caught him square in the stomach. They soared through the black air, over Calum's head and bombed the water.

Tom tried to hold him, to grip the hand that held the weapon, but in the tumble of flailing arms and legs and the crash of the waves, he lost the squirming beast.

Spitting seawater, eyes pierced by hot needles, Tom found the bottom and stood. The world was black, the map no more. He staggered to the water's edge, pebbles rolling back and forth in the unstoppable surf.

And as his night vision returned, he saw them.

Silas loomed over Calum as the injured man crawled across the beach. The sound drew Tom and Katriana to the one-sided battle.

They converged on the fight as the rod lashed Calum with another blow to the head, the cruel light, the burning flesh; hellish visions of unrelenting pain. Tom and Katriana leapt on the man but Silas, powered by insanity, stopped for nothing.

Silas whirled on them as they struck, the lightning slamming Tom back.

And Tom remembered its power.

It was not just the agony, not just the damage to skin and nerve. It tore through his body, paralysing convulsions that rendered him helpless.

Floundering for control, Tom pulled himself to the beach again, hauling handfuls of pebble and stone. To his right, Silas continued to strike the helpless giant. Tom ran his hands across the hazy ground searching for a heavy rock, anything that would make a solid, weighty weapon. He picked up the largest and stood. The smooth egg fitted easily in his palm, but it was too light - inadequate. Still, he had to try. Moving forward, fighting for strength, his left foot stumbled on something and he fell again.

Shaking, frustrated, Tom ran his hand over the cold object and, like a synesthetic, imagined its redness.

He recognised the thing immediately, the feel - the memory of it. The fuel-can he had seen on the bottom of the boat, now another piece of jetsam. Staggering upright, he grabbed the container by its handle. At last, a weapon worthy of the name. Solid, heavy and dangerous, the reassuring slop of fluid added to its mass. Thrilling to its heft, Tom gripped the handle as though he held an ancient, deadly mace. With one smooth turn, the boy swung his body in a wide circle, his arms rising like a hammer-thrower. He threw himself at Silas, loosing the weapon, connecting can and shoulder, the sound of the man's crunching bone, loud and wonderful.

Silas bellowed. Tiny compared to Calum, the man's scream was, for all his size, that of a wounded bear. Unable to stop, Tom stumbled and fell close to Katriana and the water's edge. Somehow, despite his injury, Silas was still standing, enraged and in pain. He turned towards Tom and, one arm hanging loose, closed the gap between them.

Tom reached up instinctively as the rod struck. He grabbed it, fingers curling metal, the metal spitting fire through his skin and out through his soaking hide to the black and bright Earth.

He wanted to get up but couldn't. His body was useless, twitching, his legs beyond control. Silas struck him again and again, but as the boy began to drift, his attacker stepped back, panting hard, his voice a low, steady growl.

'Not so easy, boy. Stay with us. Watch.'

Beside him, Katriana moaned softly. Silas, taking his time, lowered the tip of his rod to her cheek and cocked his head as she screamed.

Tom could not move and Calum, barely feet away, was dying. Flashes of incandescent blue leapt between the two figures, the sizzle and smell of cooking flesh tore through the air, everything else dulled to the sickening stench.

Tom struggled, control of his muscles slowly returning. The man was silent now, prodding the girl like a child poking an insect with a stick.

In the darkness beyond the macabre scene, Calum moved. He grappled for a weapon, his actions slow, his strength gone. Tom sensed a father's despair as he listened to Silas torture his daughter. The man knew that he would never stand again, never walk, never breathe the sweet air of freedom or taste the love of family he fought so hard to protect and he would never see his daughter again. Ever.

FIFTY FOUR

The whole thing had probably lasted seconds and not the interminable age that dragged through Tom's mind as he lay listening to Katriana cry for help.

He heard Calum move through the heavy fog surrounding him, trying to rise before falling back to the beach again. An ineffectual rock, thrown Tom supposed by the crippled giant, plonked close to Silas. Outlined by sporadic and brilliant forks, the attacker leaned to one side, his shoulder a misshapen mass that seemed little more than an inconvenience that would soon pass. Katriana's cries softened and Tom felt the disruptive flow of electricity wane in his body.

Tom was barely aware of anything beyond the need to help the girl, barely aware that every time he moved towards Silas, the man lashed out and brought him down again, twitching - an instant, barely-human, wreck.

Tom searched for a way out. He thought of his powers. *Dreamwords*. He could travel through time.

Apparently.

He was powerful.

And yet, at that moment, he was a baby. Useless.

He brought them to him. *The words*. A swarm, immersing and surrounding him: Creggan, sea and air. But he was fuddled, had no idea what to look for.

Somewhere, in that system or outside, he smelled something familiar. He looked at all these links waiting for him - every answer there ever was at his mental finger-tips. But still he had no idea where to go, what to look for.

A noise, definitely in the world of pain outside, snapped him back to life.

Calum hauled himself hand over fist along the ground towards his daughter, towards the creature mutilating her - blow after blow after blow.

Tom struggled to join him - to help. If they reached Silas together, they might be able to stop him.

Tom had not sensed the smell of the sea when it was there or noticed the confusing aroma of barbecued beef dull to match the faded scent of salt and air. But now they were gone, he noticed the change, his hazy mind drifting in and out of consciousness, swinging from dream to now and back again.

Silas, drenched and demonic, at last saw Calum crawling his way.

He looked at the beaten man, face-down a few yards from Tom and the girl.

Silas laughed. He actually laughed.

A part of Tom he could not reach, a place, a Being, more determined, stronger, than the weak body he occupied, picked up a stone and threw it. Silas swung his head, saw Tom and ignored him. He closed on the giant, taking his time, enjoying his moment of supreme power. Inch by inch he closed the gap. Tom could read Silas, feel the man's rage curdle the air. He would kill Calum now. It was time.

Silas stood over Katriana's father. Consumed by madness, he prepared the final swipe that would put an end to the annoyance at his feet.

Calum, pathetic, lost, reached out, his hand trembling in the gloom. Tom saw this and realised that the first hint of dawn was dulling the night. Silas looked at his foot, watching curiously as Calum gripped the insulated boot at his ankle and he chuckled. He brought the rod down hard and fast.

Tom watched, with grim resignation.

The smell.

The smell.

He knew it. It ripped through the fog. Strong. Stinging his nostrils. Familiar. Commonplace.

And as Silas struck, he recognised it too. Driving through his insanity, his crazed and frenetic attack, he understood too late that he had missed the one thing that could kill him. His own obsessive cruelty.

Tom recognised the smell, the pungent claw of petrol in his nostrils, the back of his throat. He saw a hint of red - the can -

behind Calum's crawling trail and as the rod found its home, Silas screamed a belated recognition. The arc leapt from its tip to the giant's disfigured face. Tom thought he saw Calum's white teeth flash a final smile. Silas leapt back but, caught by the ankle, he fell.

Calum, the strength of a lifetime focused in this one final act, brought both hands forward as the fuel ignited.

Covered from head to toe in gasoline, he burst into flames. Silent but for the whoomph of ignition and the hiss of tortured water, Katriana's father continued his slow, indefatigable crawl, hand-over-hand up Silas' leg. Silas screamed, kicked, clawed the pebbled shore to escape the pain. His rod was gone, his clothes ablaze.

Katriana remained, thankfully, unconscious.

Calum and Silas were one now, together, pushing back the remains of the night in a giant, writhing fireball. Silas' screams deafened everything. There was no surf, no mountain stream, no scratch of pebble on stone - only the blood-chilling sound of a torturer echoing the throes of past victims.

Tom, recovering by the second, crawled and knelt and then finally stood. It was too late. He knew it was too late but still, so close to the sea, he scooped handfuls of water, threw it like spit on a furnace onto the flaming embrace. He took the can, now empty and filled it with cool, clear sea. Everything he did seemed to take forever and with every second, every scorch of his skin, the futility of it all threatened to crush his spirit. Still he fought on. And finally, the remains charred beyond recognition, Tom doused the flames.

FIFTY FIVE

Tom carried Katriana to the cottage, her arms dead swans floating at her sides. He placed her on the settee and retrieved the remnants of the serum from Calum's room. Barely five drops remained. Filling a small glass with cold water, Tom emptied the precious fluid into it, rinsing the phial over and over again to wash every last molecule into the mix. He moved with speed but infinite care, bathing her wounds, dabbing the runny lotion over every cut and burn he could find. Her eyes flickered beneath her lids and Tom dripped the liquid onto her lips, relieved as she licked them dry in her troubled stupor. He repeated the action again and again until the glass was empty.

There was nothing he could do for her father. But he had to get help. Reluctant to leave her alone, the boy suddenly wondered how Silas had got to Creggan. Perhaps he had a boat. Surely Tom would have seen or heard him if they'd followed the same route over the mountain. Refilling the glass with clean water from the kitchen, he looked out to sea, searching for a vessel.

He saw and heard it at the same time, the raw charge of it through the water refuelling the adrenalin in his veins.

He was about to run outside, call for help, when he recognised the police insignia tattooing the side of the launch. It powered towards them, twin arcs of white foam jutting from its bow.

Tom was ecstatic. Help had arrived and Katriana would soon be in hospital.

But he would not be with her.

Ducking to the side of the window, he stared at the thing, cursed the one person he did not want to see. Dressed in his dark uniform, chequered-banded hat in hand, Chief Inspector Howard looked straight at the cottage and Tom's hair prickled on the back of his neck.

He ran to Katriana, kissed her gently on her forehead and squeezed her hands in his. As he did, unplanned and without the aid of Silas or the chair, the two shared a brief connection. For a moment they were one again, standing close together on Corven. It happened so unexpectedly that Tom stood there, his mouth open, unsure what to say to her. The girl was distressed, her movements agitated.

'I have to go,' he told her at last. She was clearly bewildered and Tom heard all the questions bubbling through her thoughts. *Where was her father? Was it all a dream? An awful nightmare?*

But the girl knew. Tom sensed this despite her desperate hope. A single tear bloomed and fell. 'He's dead, isn't he?' she whispered.

Tom took her hands and nodded his head slowly. 'I'm sorry, Katriana.'

She did not pull away.

'He loved you so much. He saved you. You were everything to him. His life.'

Katriana drew close and they held each other, her body shaking gently.

Reluctant, aware that he had seconds to move, Tom drew back and looked at her beautiful, tragic eyes. 'Goodbye,' he said. Katriana remained silent and slowly, painfully, they drifted apart.

Tom looked at her lying on the settee, still unconscious, tears streaking her face, her body shaking as she lay there.

Voices.

Tom opened the back window and slipped into the new dawn. Hiding in the bracken, he worked his way up the hill, through the ruin that had once been his home and opened the cave entrance, closing it silently behind him.

And there he stayed until the helicopter arrived and took the girl away.

*

The graveyard was quiet, the grass damp from recent rain.

The stone was simple, a granite upright slab with her name chiselled onto it. Overhead, a small bird serenaded them from a low branch and a slab of grey cloud masked the sky.

Tom reached into his pocket and brought out the heart-shaped stone. He leaned forward and lay on his side on the grave, hugging his knees for comfort.

Kathleen Henderson 1852-1887. There was no further inscription, no mention of family. She died alone. Guilt pressed on the boy as though the air had turned as leaden as the sky. He had not been there for her. All those years she had cared for them, put herself between Silas and the children, and they had simply left. Tess and Tom had one day vanished, leaving her alone with Silas.

Tom closed his eyes and journeyed to Creggan, felt himself whirl in his mother's arms, saw her writing on the beach, heard her sing her lullabies.

And his thoughts drifted and he saw the woman age before her time, isolated, living her final years watching the sea, praying for their return. Tom wanted to lash out, but who could he blame? Silas was gone, justice, in part, was served.

But was it? He brought the stone to his lips and felt its cool touch on his skin. He imagined Kathleen lying beneath the ground where he lay, saw her as she was; beautiful and strong.

He would have to move soon. They would find him here and he could not allow that. Not while his sister was out there and alone.

Behind him, beyond the stone wall of the churchyard, a car entered the village, its soft whirr stirring the present back to life.

It was time.

He stood, turned his attention to Tess and sensed her immediately. She was confused. Doing things she did not want to do. She needed him.

Tom cradled his anger, held it close, felt its strength.

Silas, he knew, was only an instrument, he and his sister slaves.

Never again would he allow himself to be used. Never again would he abandon his blood and flesh.

And as he closed the gate and faded into the hills, he felt, in some precious compartment, that distant union with Katriana, still strong, still powerful, and he wondered if he would ever see her again.

Tom looked to the East, shook the bones of the past from his mind and watched the sphere of light drift slowly towards him. He turned his thoughts to the future. To his sister.

He remembered now – drew it near. The sphere accelerated and engulfed him. Silas had taught him well.

Continued in Dreamwords Two – ***The Journal****…*

Thank you for reading the first book in the Dreamwords Series. In starting its life in audio form, Tom's story needed to be constrained – after all, I had to perform the voices. With an audience that grew to over 20,000 the Scottish accent would have been a challenge for many. However, the rest of Dreamwords is not handicapped by my limited acting skills. It is a major work, a mystery and an adventure that spans the country and beyond. It bridges time too, the present connecting with the future in the Isle of Skye and an Edinburgh yet to come - all the while keeping true to the things that matter to us all: love and hate, family and power, war and peace. Here we meet new characters whose paths are bound to Tom's and to each other. Their journeys merge - their separate stories part of a greater whole that weaves itself to shape a world that is being seeded even as you read this page.

The next three parts are complete and together constitute a single novel: Dreamwords Book Two – *The Journal.* To help you decide if this should be published, I include the first part of The Journal in the following pages.

***

Born with a terrible birthmark on his face, Jack Burns is shunned from his first day at school and stared at as he walks alone through the streets of his home town Edinburgh. When he discovers a book fused with the cliff beneath Edinburgh Castle, he is thrown into the media spotlight and linked to a strange story of two infants found inside the castle grounds over sixteen years before. One of them, a boy, had a birthmark like Jack's and the other, a girl, is buried in Greyfriar's Cemetery. Soon, a series of nightmare events leads to a fight with Tess – a sister he never knew - and Jack is propelled into a medieval future where he begins to uncover his true nature. There, he finds his first love and the strength to take on an army in a fight for freedom. With twenty thousand soldiers set against Jack and his seven friends, the boy's unique physiology is all that stands between Heaven and Hell on Earth - but he is ready. This is what he was made for.

Dreamwords Book Two – An Extract

The Journal

I am told that time-travel screws the mind. And yet, if I stay, I am as dead as the others. Perhaps if I had space to think I would not go. Would dementia ease the pain? A part of me wants to sleep where I fall. Let the creeping sickness bring peace.

Enough!

This is a journal, of sorts, automated by my thoughts on an ancient book – insurance against a blank mind. I know little enough now and five minutes could surely answer many questions, but an audience of corpses spurs me on. Everything is corrupted, in my head and beyond reach. The facts that led me here are elusive, but only one thing matters. The children are our future.

I have forty five seconds to finish this brief to myself.

If I survive the journey, I need to know the who, the what, the when and the why of it all. Perhaps there are clues in the past, in the time before the disease, before we learned to fear Dreamwords. What follows is scavenged from the voyage I am about to make, my thoughts cast like a net through the ether. The tricks of distance and of time, the uncertainty of the search criteria, and the limits of damage to my brain, will make it what it is. Right now, it is all I can hope for.

Two seconds.

And the children - I do not even know their names...

From the distilled thoughts of Jack Burns – Date ambiguous

I saw her on the summit of Arthur's Seat. Below me, Edinburgh was as grey as my thoughts. I had crept from the house before my parents awoke and now watched the city's neon glow fade from the underside of the cloud-base, leaving it drained of colour. District by district, rosaries of light disappeared and the houses and streets emerged from the night as would an old photo in a tray of liquid. The air was cold and I was dressed in shorts and tee-shirt, but I did not notice.

I was five years old.

I hugged myself, looking for comfort wherever I could find it. The previous day had been my first at school and the worst of my life. I could not understand what had changed to make my appearance so frightening to those around me. Too young to understand, I thought, at first that my condition had worsened, and later, when I stood on a stool to examine my left cheek in the bathroom mirror, I saw nothing that had not been there the last time I had looked. To my young eyes, the red stain was as normal as my nose or my father's ears, but I was learning fast. Until that day, when nervous children lined up to take their first assembly, I had met mostly adults and was unaware of the effect my appearance had on people. Then, standing in the middle of a line of my peers, the girl next to me, Claire Thompson, started screaming and moved back as her eyes widened and her nose streamed with snot. All around her, others followed, the contagion of hysteria sweeping the line until I was left silent and alone in the centre of a circle. Mrs Crow, the duty teacher, scooped me in her arms and took me inside while another adult soothed the chaos I had started. I remember the smell of tobacco in her hair.

I remained silent as the teacher asked my name, and then, when I refused to answer, she said; "It's Jack, isn't it? Jack Burns." Still I said nothing. And so the pattern for school was set. On that day, sitting at the front of the class, I was the only child who did not cry, even as I felt a crowd of eyes stare at my back. My silence was not unusual and that evening, when my parents asked me how I had enjoyed the adventure of my first day in school, I shrugged my shoulders and told them it was fine, but that, no, I did not meet any new friends.

I had no idea what compelled me to rise that morning and tiptoe from the house and I did not think about the anguish I would cause if either of my parents found my bed empty when they awoke.

Throughout the night I had watched them in my dreams; the circle of children calling for mothers to save them from the monster in their midst. Dreams, for me, are special. Sometimes I know I'm dreaming and sometimes I don't, but always I am engulfed by them. They are as real as anything experienced with my eyes wide open - sight, touch, smell, fear, laughter and colour – everything vivid, the details scalpel sharp.

Perhaps I was simply escaping or perhaps I had left to meet the woman who was to change my life. Perhaps it was just time.

In the grey light, the castle washed into the background, painted by a hand skilled in camouflage. Somewhere in the distance a dog barked and somewhere else a faraway door slammed. Unlike my dreams, Edinburgh, that morning, was muted.

When she first appeared, I thought she was my mother and wondered briefly how she had known where I was. She had the same pale complexion and soft wavy hair as my mother and her slim figure moved with a grace that could have matched a dancer's. But as I tilted my head to look at her face, she seemed to soar forever upward, contrasting sharply with my mother's diminutive stature so that I was momentarily bemused by the attention she gave me. Her eyes defied the rule of the morning and sparkled bright blue and I noticed nothing else as she silently sat by my side. Transfixed by her, I watched as she tucked her knees to her chin, wrapped her arms around her shins and turned to the city. Moments later I did the same and together we watched as life leaked from the houses and onto the streets. I forgot about the children and I forgot about my disfigurement and for a time I was no longer alone.

It did not occur to me that she should not be there or that her attachment to me could have been sinister. It was enough to know that she demanded nothing and did not flinch when she looked at me. Time drifted slowly and an early morning jogger grunted past us, over the rocky top and down the other side. His sweat-banded head was angled to the ground and I'm not sure he saw us as he dripped his way along the path.

When we could no longer hear the rattle of stones beneath his feet the woman spoke quietly and without taking her eyes from the view: "I'm here to help you."

I looked at her, but she continued her vigil on the city. A small strand of hair escaped the tight flow and danced with the breeze until it became lodged between her lips. I asked her her name.

"Muria," she said and pulled the hair free as she spoke.

That small action seemed to stir a memory that I could not grasp. She was a stranger and yet familiar. I was drawn to her; trusted her without knowing why. With the innocence of a five-year-old, I took her hand when she stood. Together, we walked down the hill towards a new day.

*

After that morning, I did not see Muria for another two years, but I never forgot her. On that day, she walked me home and knelt on one knee at the garden gate, penetrating my mind with her steady gaze. "I have something for you," she said. Obediently, I held out my hands as she proffered a clenched fist. "This," she said, as she unfurled her long fingers, "is a magic stone." My hands bounced as they took the weight of the heavy pebble, its smooth grey surface warm to the touch. I brought it to my face and pressed it to my cheek and held it there, rolling my head from side to side to feel the power of it.

"What does it do?" I asked.

"It's invisible," she told me.

I brought it down and stared at the object in amazement. Indistinguishable from a million others, it shone in my eyes as though it was the most precious of precious stones that had ever existed.

"No-one but you can see it. Keep it with you at all times."

When I told her that it was too big to carry everywhere, Muria said that it was not. When I looked again, the stone was smaller and I cupped it in my palm and thrust it into my pocket.

"Whenever you feel frightened, Jack," she said. "Take the stone and hold it tightly in your hand."

"But what does it do?"

"The stone, Jack, is your strength."

I felt the round surface reassuring in my pocket.

"If you so decide, you can throw the stone and kill anyone you choose."

I reeled back at her words and dropped the weapon in my pocket as though it was on fire. But as she continued, my hand, unguided by me, found it again and the heat was no longer frightening.

"This is important Jack. You have a grave responsibility. Use the stone only when you must."

Across the road, a small Scottie dog dragged an old man on a tight leash, but I only noticed because the man scolded the animal in a high pitched whine that penetrated Muria's hypnotic grip. She brought me back. "You must be brave, Jack. Other children do not understand. It is not their fault."

I nodded my head vigorously and was taken aback when the image of the girl who had started the raucous at school suddenly popped into my head. She was lying in a pool of blood, her head opened like a split tomato. Muria was there too and her eyes burned into mine and I felt terrible shame for what I had done. Muria held my attention and the scene vanished around her and we were back at the garden gate. She did not mention the vision we had shared, but simply said. "The truly powerful do not hurt others, Jack. Remember that."

She did not say goodbye, but was suddenly gone. I stood there for some minutes before the cold forced me to move. I turned to the house, walked to the door and opened it. Back in my bedroom, and two minutes after covering myself with the duvet, my father's alarm clock buzzed through the thin wall. My second day at school was about to begin.

Thank you for your honesty.

www.dreamwords.com